Caribbean Island Hospital

Twin docs in paradise!

Welcome to the US Virgin Islands! Home to doctors Matthew and Marcus Oleson. Matthew and Marcus may be twins, but they couldn't be *more* different. Their passion for treating patients and saving lives might just be the only thing that they have in common! Until a surgeon and a nurse burst into their hearts...and Matthew and Marcus find that they have falling in love in common, too!

Escape to the Caribbean with...

Reunited with Her Surgeon Boss

A Ring for His Pregnant Midwife

Available now!

Dear Reader,

Thank you for picking up a copy of *Reunited with Her Surgeon Boss*, which is book one of Caribbean Island Hospital.

I dreamed of this duet a couple of years ago. Matthew and his twin, Marcus, walked into my head fully formed, and I'm so glad I get to share their stories with you.

Victoria grew up in the foster system, alone, and didn't trust her heart with anyone. She fell in love once but pushed it away for her career. However, she's never stopped dreaming of that man who got through her defenses.

Matthew is no stranger to heartache after losing his wife to cancer. He isn't going to ever put his heart on the line again, until the woman he first fell in love with comes back into his hospital.

Matthew and Victoria have to put old hurts to the side to complete a complicated surgery, but love always finds a way and they both find themselves losing their hearts under a tropical moon.

I hope you enjoy Victoria and Matthew's story.

I love hearing from readers, so please drop by my website, www.amyruttan.com, or give me a shout on Twitter, @ruttanamy.

With warmest wishes,

Amy Ruttan

REUNITED WITH HER SURGEON BOSS

AMY RUTTAN

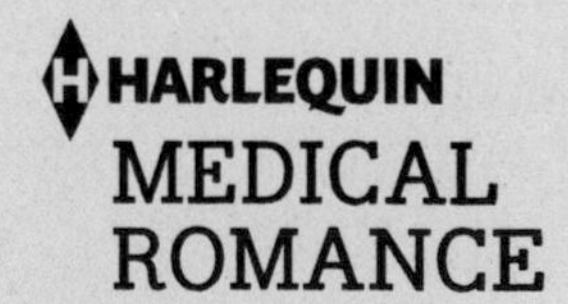

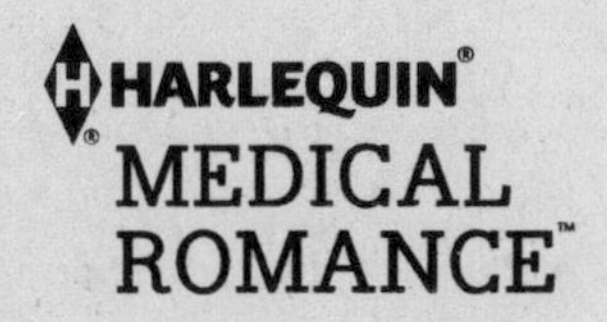

Recycling programs for this product may not exist in your area.

ISBN-13: 978-1-335-40919-5

Reunited with Her Surgeon Boss

This edition published by arrangement with Harlequin Books S.A.

For questions and comments about the quality of this book, please contact us at CustomerService@Harlequin.com.

Harlequin Enterprises ULC
22 Adelaide St. West, 41st Floor
Toronto, Ontario M5H 4E3, Canada
www.Harlequin.com

Printed in U.S.A.

Born and raised just outside Toronto, Ontario, **Amy Ruttan** fled the big city to settle down with the country boy of her dreams. After the birth of her second child, Amy was lucky enough to realize her lifelong dream of becoming a romance author. When she's not furiously typing away at her computer, she's mom to three wonderful children, who use her as a personal taxi and chef.

Books by Amy Ruttan

Harlequin Medical Romance

First Response

Pregnant with the Paramedic's Baby

Cinderellas to Royal Brides

Royal Doc's Secret Heir

Carrying the Surgeon's Baby
The Surgeon's Convenient Husband
Baby Bombshell for the Doctor Prince
Reunited with Her Hot-Shot Surgeon
A Reunion, a Wedding, a Family
Twin Surprise for the Baby Doctor
Falling for the Billionaire Doc
Falling for His Runaway Nurse

Visit the Author Profile page
at Harlequin.com for more titles.

For all those dreaming of a second chance
and a happily-ever-after.

Praise for
Amy Ruttan

"*Baby Bombshell for the Doctor Prince* is an emotional swoon-worthy romance…. Author Amy Ruttan beautifully brought these two characters together, making them move towards their happy ever after. Highly recommended for all readers of romance."

—*Goodreads*

CHAPTER ONE

YOU'RE OKAY. This is a minor setback. You've handled worse before. And who wouldn't want to work in paradise?

And that's what Dr. Victoria Jensen had to keep telling herself. This was a good thing. It was an opportunity.

Even though she felt alone again.

Scared, but she wasn't going to let anyone see that part of her. She'd kept that part hidden since her mother died. As she had no other biological family, she'd grown up in the foster system from the age of ten, bounding from home to home. No one had ever wanted to adopt her, so she'd locked her heart away.

She'd also learned she could either shy away and be a pushover or she could fight for her life.

She chose to fight.

And she chose to help by saving lives.

No one had been there for her growing up, and she didn't want anyone else to feel alone the way she had. Being a surgeon gave her the opportunity to help others while also giving her the perfect excuse to keep people at a distance. A career that would keep her too busy to even think about committing to a lifetime with just one person. It was better to be a lone wolf. Your heart never had to be on the line if it was just you.

Being a surgeon was what she'd always wanted. Even when she couldn't always control the outcome.

Which brought her back to why she was here.

She'd lost a patient.

A very important patient. A foreign ambassador to the US.

The hospital's board of directors had suggested she take a leave of absence until the autopsy findings were released and the media interest died down, and though she hadn't wanted to agree, she hadn't been given a choice.

The timing had been fortuitous, though, as her mentor, Dr. Paul Martin, had been asked to go to St. Thomas in the US Virgin Islands to assist with a domino kidney transplant surgery, and Paul had arranged for her to go in his place.

She'd lost patients before and it always stung, but this patient had the press hounding her.

Blaming her.

On assignment in the US Virgin Islands, she could lie low, do her work and wait for the attention to die down.

It was the perfect plan, in theory.

She straightened her white lab coat as she stared at her reflection in the mirror in the women's washroom and shook away the last tendrils of self-doubt that were swirling around in her brain. Her palms were sweaty, and she hadn't slept much the night before, but that didn't matter.

She could shake this off and prove to this hospital that they were damn lucky to have one of the best transplant surgeons working for them. Even for a short time.

Inwardly she cringed at her pep talk. It was something her mentor, Paul, had taught her when she became his resident. Paul had taught her to be confident. To think for herself and exude confidence, which she knew often made her come across as cold-blooded and arrogant.

Be a shark, he'd say—*it's the only way to survive.*

He was cool, detached and only looked out for his career and those of the few students he deemed were worthy to be taught by him.

She had been one of them, and for the first time in her life, she had been chosen by someone. It was Dr. Paul Martin who had told her to not get bogged down by a family or love. She had understood that all too well living in the foster system.

Except there were parts of her that didn't like that. There were secret parts of her that wanted love, security and tenderness.

It was something she had wanted ever since she'd lost her mom.

But she only had herself.

She was the only person who had never let herself down…until she agreed to do the ambassador's surgery against her better judgment.

In the ten years she'd been a transplant surgeon, nothing had gone as catastrophically bad as the operation that had made her flee New York. And it wasn't even her fault. She hadn't wanted to do the transplant surgery. The ambassador wasn't in a fit state for the operation, and though she told her superiors that the surgery needed to wait, no one had listened.

A chain of events with an unstable patient had unfolded, and though she'd tried everything she could, he'd started to crash on her table. Just when she thought she'd managed to stabilize him and that the transplant might finally take, there'd been a blood clot from the suture line that she couldn't evacuate, which had ended it all.

The ambassador died.

So here she was in this island paradise, somewhere she could work in peace. Even though New York City was all that mattered and was where her life was, this would be a good change of pace.

The hospital here needed help running a complicated domino surgery for multiple patients who needed kidney transplants.

A domino was for those who needed a kidney and had someone willing to donate but wasn't compatible with their volunteer donor. So each pair—donor and recipient—were matched with someone else waiting for a kidney who was incompatible with their own willing donor. There were a lot of moving pieces, and it required coordination. Each participant was in a chain, much like a set of dominoes, and if one piece dropped out, the whole thing fell apart.

It could be a logistical nightmare for those unfamiliar with it, but thankfully she'd done domino surgeries before.

Before she got started, though, she needed to meet the new chief of surgery, which was the main thing currently causing her anxiety. The previous chief—the one who had agreed to her coming in Paul's place—was Paul's friend, but he'd had to take early retirement for personal reasons, and she didn't know who the new chief of surgery was. She'd been talking to Paul about it last night, but their call had dropped out and she'd missed the name.

There was a part of her that wondered if the new chief would be wary about her.

If they were a sensible surgeon they'd see that what happened wasn't your fault. They would know about the complication. They would get it.

Victoria might be a talented surgeon, but she wasn't God, and there was no way she could've stopped that blood clot from forming.

And if it wasn't for the press unfairly blaming her, she'd still be in New York.

Yeah, and miserable.

Victoria shook that sneaky little thought from her head.

You don't need anyone else.

Victoria adjusted her brown hair, which was tied back in a bun, except the humidity kept causing strands to escape. Once everything about her appearance was controlled, sterile and clean, she washed her hands and then nodded curtly to the reflection in the mirror and left the women's washroom.

The chief of surgery's office was at the end of the hall. Each step from her heels seemed to beat in time with her heart, and she tried to swallow the lump in her throat.

Come on. You can do this.

"Dr. Jensen?" the chief's assistant—Yvonne, according to her name tag—asked as she approached the office.

"Yes. I'm here to see the chief of surgery."

Yvonne nodded and smiled brightly. "Just a moment. I'll check with Dr. Olesen to see if he's ready for you."

Yvonne stood up and slipped in the office behind her desk.

Victoria frowned and worried her bottom lip. Dr. Olesen? Surely it was a different Dr. Olesen. There were a lot of Dr. Olesens out there. Fate wouldn't be that cruel as to put her in the hands of her old rival from her residency days.

Matthew Olesen had been the only man who had ever gotten under her skin. The only resident in their surgical program to be a threat. He drove her crazy, and she had been crazy attracted to him. He had made her blood sing with pleasure.

He had been her first. They had spent so many nights together, and she'd fallen for him.

Hard.

She'd fallen in love with him.

And even though she wanted more, she'd been scared by the intensity of their passion. She was scared of trusting him and putting her heart in someone's hands.

There had been only one position to work with Dr. Paul Martin in transplant surgery, and she'd wanted it.

Nothing was going to get in her way.

Not even a man she loved…

"You really want to end things like this?" Matt asked, his hands on her shoulders.

She tried to shrug out of his embrace but couldn't bring herself to pull away from him.

She really didn't want to end things, but

this was better for her heart. She had plans, and Matt didn't fit in those plans. It was hard to walk away from him, to break the delicious connection when all she wanted was more of him, but she was too scared to risk her heart.

There was no way she could have both Matt and the career she'd worked so hard for.

Love was too complicated.

"Yes. I'm taking the job. There's one spot and it's mine."

Matt let go of her shoulders, and she suddenly felt cold.

"You're breaking my heart, Victoria. It's you I want."

She swallowed back the tears that were threatening to spill. She didn't cry in front of anyone.

"I don't want you, Matt. For me, this has always been about the job. That's all that matters. Nothing else."

Except it was a lie.

She did want him.

His gaze hardened, and his spine stiffened. "Fine. Then I won't bother you again."

It had hurt, but she'd gotten over it.

Have you?

She'd thought he would stay in New York, but he hadn't.

Matthew hadn't tried to fight for her, and she'd gotten the message. She was on her own. And that was fair. It was what she was used to. She was used to people leaving her, and she could deal.

She couldn't rely on anyone but herself.

Have you really gotten over it?

Dr. Matthew Olesen had disappeared from her radar, and she'd never bothered to look him up. It hurt too much, because as much as she wanted to tell herself she was over him, she wasn't. There was a part of her that still yearned for him and wanted him, but she'd ruined it, and so instead she'd focused solely on her career. She'd dated other men, but no one had ever held a candle to Matt.

No one made her heart beat faster. No one made her body tremble with pleasure with one simple look from his blue, blue eyes. Matthew still owned that small hidden part of her heart that she kept to herself.

You need to get control of yourself.

Yvonne came out of the office. "He's ready to see you now."

Victoria nodded and opened the door, holding her breath as she stepped into the room.

Her hands were shaking and she was sweating like crazy, hoping that no one could see it.

It wasn't Matthew.

It couldn't be him.

His back was to her as he was typing on his computer. His hair was short, caramel colored, and she couldn't tell much from the back of his head. She stood there, the tension filling the room as she waited for him to turn around and look at her.

Fate wasn't this cruel.

Look at me, she silently screamed in her head. She wanted to be put out of her misery.

"You've come a long way, yes?"

The voice was a bit deeper than she remembered, but it slid down her spine with that tendril of familiarity that sent a shiver of dread and a zing of anticipation racing through her. Her stomach did a flip, knowing what it was like when that voice whispered sweet nothings in her ear as she melted for him.

Oh, God. Not him.

This was like some kind of sick joke.

She was in hell and being punished.

He turned, and her heart skipped a beat as she looked into the crystal-blue eyes of the only man who had ever made her swoon.

The man she'd let walk away. The only man she'd ever loved.

The man who still haunted her dreams, taunting her with something she could never have. Victoria didn't believe in happily-ever-afters, but a part of her always regretted and wondered if she could've had one with him.

And her body was still reacting to him. Even after all this time.

Traitor.

"Dr. Olesen," she said curtly, trying to swallow the hard lump that was threatening to choke off her air supply.

He smiled, but that smile didn't reach his eyes. It was cold, detached and hurt, and in trying to avoid his gaze, she noticed the wedding band on his finger. Not that she should be surprised, Matt had always wanted to get married and have a family, and she hadn't. Or at least she'd told him she didn't.

There was a part of her, deep down, that secretly longed for those things. But she knew they were just pipe dreams and were not meant to be hers.

Only because you're too scared to have those things.

"Dr. Jensen." He tented his fingers and

looked at her, a look that chilled her to the bone. “I never expected or wanted to have to see your face again. But here we are.”

CHAPTER TWO

IT WAS A LIE. He did want to see her again. For years he'd longed for her, even though she had made it clear she didn't want him when she ended things. She'd chosen a job over him, and he was still hurt over that.

There had been many years, many nights when she haunted him. Like some kind of ghost that had a hold on his soul. She'd possessed him for so long, it was a battle to put the memories of her to rest.

Then he'd met Kirsten two years after he left New York. She was a breath of fresh air. She'd made him feel like he could open his heart again. She'd taught him he could love, and he'd married her thinking they'd have a long and happy life together.

It wasn't meant to be, though, as cancer had reared its ugly head and Kirsten's life had been cut too short.

His heart had been shattered far too often. The only thing he cared about now was his job. Since Kirsten had died, he'd thrown his all into his work to try and drown out the pain. For the last five years, he'd been so focused, and it had finally paid off.

He was now chief of surgery at Ziese Memorial Hospital and just in time for a delicate and tricky domino surgery. Matthew had made plans to find only the best transplant surgeon he could to coordinate the surgery, but then he saw that his predecessor had already picked a surgeon just before he left for his early retirement.

And it was the one surgeon Matthew never wanted to see again.

His own personal demon.

Dr. Victoria Jensen.

And seeing her in person now, it was like time hadn't touched her. It was like he was staring at that same woman who had owned his heart and soul ten years ago. The same woman who took his heart and crushed it between her well-manicured fingers.

Her dark hair was pulled back in that severe bun now, but he could still recall how soft her hair was when she let it down. How it naturally curled around her heart-shaped face and how silky it felt when he ran his hands through it.

Her lips were still full and pink—they had been lips that were made for kissing, if there was such a thing as lips made just for kissing. And her eyes were large, brown and expressive. One moment they could be glazed over in passion and the next it was as though hellfire were burning in the depths of them.

He much preferred the pleasure in her eyes, especially when he was running his hands over her luscious curves, her body trembling from his touch.

Just thinking about all those memories that he had banished ten years ago fired his blood, and he was annoyed that he was letting himself think of her like that again.

There had been a part of him that wanted to put a stop to her coming and cancel the contract that had been signed for the next month, but he knew that Victoria was one of the best transplant surgeons in North America who would be an asset to the surgery.

And the surgery was in shambles, and he needed help.

There were patients and donors, but that was it. There was no coordination. Not many labs had been run, no prep. Nothing was organized.

It was chaos.

His predecessor had made the right choice in offering the position to her, but the only thing that Matthew couldn't figure out was why?

Why did she leave that amazing position and job in Manhattan to come to St. Thomas? He was pretty sure that it really had nothing to do with the domino surgery. Matthew had done part of his residency there—he knew that they often saw surgeries like this in New York.

So, why had she come?

Perhaps it was the death of the ambassador?

He knew better than most that no matter how hard you tried to save them, patients sometimes died during surgery. It happened.

He might have been harsh to her, but he needed to keep his distance from her. He needed to keep her at arm's length. And if she was the Victoria he remembered, he knew she could handle this domino on her own.

He had to be careful.

He had to be cold and detached.

He had to be harsh, so that he didn't fall

into that same trap that he had before when he had been young and foolish.

"I'm sorry you feel that way," Victoria said stiffly, breaking through his conflicted thoughts. "I don't want to be here working with you. So I don't like this situation, either."

"Don't you?" he asked under his breath.

Her cheeks bloomed in crimson, and he swore that he could see the flames of anger dancing in her eyes.

Maybe he had pushed her a bit too far.

"No. I don't. Look, I don't want to get into what happened between us. The past is the past and I'm here to work. That is, if you'll let me."

He grinned and leaned back in his swivel chair. "That is indeed an interesting prospect."

"What is?"

"Me letting you work here."

"Well, you are the chief," she stated, and he knew from her tone, the stiffness in her voice, that he was annoying her. Matthew was a professional and he didn't deal with other surgeons this way, but this was a unique situation.

And even though she was the best, he wasn't sure if it was the smartest thing letting her stay in St. Thomas and work with him.

This isn't like residency.

They weren't competitors. He was her boss.

It wasn't going to be like it was ten years ago. He had slept with a viper and been bitten by falling in love with her, and he wouldn't let that happen again.

Except she wasn't a snake. And it wasn't losing the job that hurt him.

Far from it. It was losing her. It was her choosing career over him when he would've chosen her over work every time.

She had been so soft in his arms. She'd melted, and he had been consumed by her. He had loved her so much.

Get ahold of yourself.

"And why wouldn't I let you work here?"

"I don't have time to play these childish games, Matthew."

"It's Dr. Olesen," he said sternly. The familiarity with which she used his name was unnerving. It felt right and natural, and he didn't like it one bit.

"I'm sorry. Dr. Olesen, then."

"You're right. I am being childish, and the past is in the past. You were hired by my predecessor, and I am willing to honor the contract. I am thankful that you chose to come here at this time."

Her eyes narrowed, and she cocked her head to one side. "I didn't choose to come here. Do you not know why I had to come here? It's all over the news!"

"The ambassador dying? What of it? I mean, it's unfortunate, but that doesn't have anything to do with my domino."

She sighed and then pursed her lips together. "You're right. But I didn't choose to come here. I was forced to come here. I needed to lie low for a while."

She knew she was being melodramatic, but so was everyone else, and she was exasperated. She was so frustrated with the press and the rest of the world believing lies about her.

There was a snowball of things that had happened during that surgery that weren't her fault, but thinking about it made her stomach twist with anxiety and her palms were sweating as she clenched her hands together, trying not to wring them.

And now Matthew was her new boss.

Matthew.

"Tell me you don't love me," he demanded.

She looked away because she couldn't look

him in the eye. Her heart was breaking, but she was terrified.

"I don't..."

"You can't even look at me, Victoria." He tipped her chin, and she melted under his touch. "Tell me you don't love me. Tell me you don't want me."

"I don't love you... I don't want you."

She had lied to Matthew then, because she had loved him, but the job was more important.

It was a lie to protect herself. She wasn't going to rely on anyone for her emotional or financial security. She'd worked so hard, to the point of exhaustion and starvation, to get herself through school. It had been stressful—there were days she couldn't eat because she had to pay for a book, and she'd sworn she would never go through that again.

Not even for love, because love could be lost.

A skill—surgical skill—was something that was always needed.

So she had had to lie to Matthew, even though their time together in New York had been one of the only happy times in her life, and there were moments when she was alone and she wondered if she had done the right thing.

The lie had done its damage. It was clear Matthew hated her, and she'd deal with it, though it stung.

"What happened, exactly?" Matthew asked calmly.

There was no censure in his voice, just professional curiosity.

She sighed in relief.

"It was a blood clot," she said.

"Walk me through it," he said gently.

Her heart skipped a beat. It was just like old times when they had been working on a case together and she would get overwhelmed. Talking it through with him had always helped. She missed this. It was calming.

"I was doing a liver and bowel transplant on the ambassador, and there was a string of complications. His blood pressure began to rise. His heart stopped. We'd get it stabilized, and then it would race. There was excessive bleeding and I got that under control, but one thing would lead to another. He went into multisystem organ failure, and a clot broke away at his suture line. I couldn't evacuate the clot in time. At that point, there was no way I could save him. I had misgivings about doing the surgery in the first place. He was too weak to handle such a major surgery."

"So why did you?"

"I was pressured by the patient. He insisted I had to do it. I shouldn't have done it."

He nodded. "Yes. I agree you shouldn't have taken on that surgery if your gut told you not to, but I don't understand something."

"What?" she asked.

"Why do you have to lie low?" There was a slight twinkle in his eyes, and she breathed another sigh of relief.

She smiled. "The press latched onto the story and were looking for a scapegoat. What they failed to realize was that the ambassador was already very ill and there were no guarantees with the surgery. If it had gone well, I could've been a hero, and because it didn't, I was handed over like a lamb to the slaughter by the press to the public. The board suggested I take the temporary position here until things die down, so I'm biding my time while we wait for the autopsy findings to be released."

Matthew's face relaxed, and she was relieved to see sympathy rather than censure or that cold detachment he'd exuded when she had first walked into his office. "I see, so that's why you left New York City."

She nodded. "For now. Out of sight, out of mind. The press will hopefully move on to something else soon."

A smile tugged on the corner of his lips, only this time it was friendly. "And you had no idea I had just been appointed as the new chief when you agreed to come here?"

Victoria let out a breath that she hadn't realized she'd been holding. "Right."

"Well, it seems we're both in a difficult situation. I'm sorry that the press has latched onto the idea that the ambassador's demise was your doing. Knowing how precarious transplant surgeries can be, I know you're not at fault. Our hospital needs you for this domino surgery. I know it's old hat for you, but here as Ziese Memorial, we don't get many surgeries that are this kind of complicated, and I would appreciate your expertise."

Victoria wasn't sure she was hearing him correctly. "You want me to stay?"

"I do," he said. "As you say, we can put the past in the past and just work together as colleagues on this, can we not?"

"Yes. We can."

"Good."

Relief washed over her, and it felt like her knees were going to give out. All she wanted to do was collapse in a great big heap. She hadn't realized how on edge and stressed she had been.

For the first time in a couple of weeks, she was being listened to and accepted.

Maybe Paul was right and she could just disappear here in paradise. Maybe this was right where she needed to be before she could return to Manhattan and her normal life.

Your lonely and boring life.

Victoria shook that thought from her head. She wasn't going to let those kinds of thoughts in right now. That wasn't important. She'd chosen her life.

She would throw herself into her work and run this domino surgery. For the next month, she could hide away and do what she loved. The only catch: she had to work with Matthew Olesen.

Or rather, work under Matthew. He was her new boss.

They weren't equals in the hierarchy here.

Maybe the universe felt she needed some humble pie and atonement for choosing her career over him. This next month would undoubtedly be punishment enough.

She could keep her distance, though.

Ten years was enough time to get over someone.

Wasn't it?

"Yes. I am grateful for you letting me work here, and I look forward to getting to know all the patients and learning the case."

"Well, no time like the present." Matthew stood up. "Come on, I'll take you down to the boardroom where we have everything set up and information about the referring physicians."

"That sounds great, Dr. Olesen."

Matthew frowned. "No. That's not right."

"You told me to call you that," she stated. "Or do you prefer that I call you Chief?"

"No. I don't really like that, either."

"So what do you want me to call you? Jerk face? I used to call you that sometimes," she teased.

There was a hint of a smile at the corner of his mouth. "No, I mean, we're pretty informal here, and I'm sorry for acting like a pain and forcing you to address me as Dr. Olesen. If we're going to work together closely, then it would seem odd to the rest of the staff that you address me like that. They would ask questions, and I like to keep my personal life private."

"Same with me. I would prefer not to talk about why I'm here. I've been subjected to enough gossip to last a lifetime."

Matthew smiled and opened the door to his office, motioning for her to leave. "Good."

Victoria stepped out of his office as he shut the door and then fell into step beside him as he quickly walked away, instantly regretting her choice of heels but keeping up with him the best she could.

There were a few turns, and she was glad that he was showing her the way, because she knew that she could easily get completely lost. As they passed people in the hall, staff would greet him and he would smile brightly and wave, but the smile didn't reach his eyes the way it used to.

That was something that she had always liked about Matthew Olesen. He smiled with his whole being, which made you want to smile, too. He made you feel like he was your friend.

It was something that she'd also envied about him.

His bedside manner when they had been residents was something everyone in their program strived to mimic, but only Matthew could pull it off.

As they walked the halls of Ziese Memorial, she could tell that something had changed—there was something different about the man she'd once known so well.

And it was then she caught the glint of gold on his finger again.

He was married. He was off-limits.

And her heart sank when it had no right to.

Why wouldn't he be married?

Matthew was too good of a man to not sweep a woman off her feet. She, herself, had been almost swept away by him. Instead, she'd tossed him aside.

The lack of sparkle might be because he had a family waiting for him and he was spread too thin. Paul always said a family was a burden and bogged you down. Held you back as a surgeon.

The last thing Matthew probably wanted to do was spend time with her and show a new employee around the halls of Ziese Memorial. He probably wanted to go home and be with his family, and she couldn't help but wonder what his kids looked like.

She knew that kids had always been in Matthew's plans, but not in hers.

Liar.

That niggling little voice reared its head.

There was a part of her that wanted kids very badly, but she was so afraid. The pain of growing up in the foster system was still a deep cut that burned. She couldn't let that happen to her kids if something ever happened to her.

Victoria shook that unwelcome and uncomfortable thought away as he stopped and opened the door to a small boardroom, where all the files were laid out and there was a blank whiteboard.

The blank whiteboard made her heart sink. By now recipients should be tested. Donors and a plan should have already been discussed.

Instead she was staring at a blank board and a stack of files.

They really weren't far in their planning of this surgery, and she only had a month to figure all this out?

She had her work cut out for her.

No wonder they needed help.

Matthew could tell that Victoria was concerned when he opened the door of the boardroom. He had had the same thoughts when he took over as chief of surgery. This domino was far behind in its planning, and at this point he wasn't even sure if they could perform such a tricky and complicated procedure in the time frame they'd been given.

There were so many moving pieces to this, and nothing was going forward. It was all at a standstill, and he knew everyone involved was frustrated.

His own brother, who had referred one of his patients from the island of St. John to be a part of this surgery, had been on the phone with him constantly about the progress of the surgery, and it was starting to wear on Matthew.

He understood how frustrating it was for a doctor who had referred a patient to have to wait. It was also bothering him because it was his twin brother, Marcus, and they didn't exactly have the best relationship.

Marcus only called when he wanted something.

You don't call him, either.

Matthew shook that thought away.

They might be identical twins, but their looks were where their similarities ended.

Marcus was younger by twenty minutes, and he was the quintessential younger sibling. He had been babied. Growing up attending boarding schools since the age of eleven, Matthew had spent a lot of time parenting Marcus rather than being his brother. It was exhausting. Even when they were in medical school, Matthew had to help him study because Marcus preferred to socialize and party. It frustrated him. Even though Marcus was a doctor, he was too laid-back, too fly-by-the-seat-of-his-pants.

Matthew liked control and planning—that's why he was a surgeon. The operating room was his happy place. Everything in its place and everything in order.

That's why Matthew was now chief of surgery at Ziese Memorial Hospital and his twin brother was living on a boat off the shore of St. John. Even if there was a small part of him that envied his brother's lifestyle—how carefree Marcus was.

Marcus didn't get too involved with women. He dated casually. Matthew couldn't do that. That wasn't his style. It had never been his style.

Matthew missed the way their relationship had been, back before puberty had hit. Before both of them became hotheaded teenagers and fell for the same girl.

That girl had been the tip of the iceberg after years of friction. She hadn't been the cause of their strain, just the catalyst.

And even though neither of them got the girl, their strained relationship continued to worsen from there. So much so that they were now practically strangers who just so happened to be biologically related.

There was no trust on either side. Only censure, coldness and hurt.

This delay in the domino certainly wasn't helping their relationship, either. Matthew wanted to help Marcus's patient and all the others, but he needed assistance.

Which was where Victoria fit in.

He shook his head and then scrubbed a hand over his face. "I know it's pretty sparse. My predecessor wasn't the most organized."

That was the understatement of the year. All the people on this list were running out of time. The surgery had to start and soon.

Victoria had picked up one of the files. "I'll say. You know there is a lot of testing that needs to be done to make sure that antibodies match? It isn't as simple as saying, 'I'll give a kidney to you,' or there wouldn't be a need for a domino surgery."

Matthew narrowed his eyes. "I am very

well aware of that. I am glad you're here, though. If I hadn't taken over the chief of surgery's duties, then I would be handling it all myself."

Victoria cocked one of her thinly arched brows. "And how many dominoes have you done?"

"What do you mean by that?" Matthew asked, bristling as he crossed his arms. "Are you implying that I'm an incompetent surgeon?"

"How did you get that from what I asked?"

"Well, I know Dr. Martin doesn't think much of our hospital. Since he was your mentor, I assumed that you thought the same," he groused.

Victoria rolled her eyes. "You assumed wrong. Besides, Dr. Martin recommended I come here in his place."

"Did he now? Would you have come here knowing I was chief?"

A blush tinged her cheeks. "I don't know."

"You must've known I came back home to the US Virgin Islands. You would've known I was here."

"That's presumptuous."

"Why?" he asked, needling her.

After the way she'd hurt him, there was a

part of him that wanted to know why she'd chosen to come here now after all this time.

"I haven't followed your surgical career since you left Manhattan, so I don't know how many dominoes you've performed. I had my own career to think of."

It stung to hear her say that, but it confirmed his thoughts. She didn't really care about him the way he had cared about her.

"When I left New York, I came to work here, and I have participated in one domino since then." He rubbed the back of his neck nervously. "It's been a while, but I am aware of how they're done."

Victoria set down the file. "I want to get to work on this right away and see if any of our patients have donors that are willing to be tested and bring them in."

"I'll help you," Matthew offered.

"I could be here until late," Victoria stated. "There's a lot of information to go through."

"So?" he asked, confused.

And then her gaze landed on his hand, where he still wore the ring. Kirsten had been gone for five years, but he just couldn't bring himself to take the ring off. And with her looking at it, it brought it all to the surface.

All those joyful memories of when he'd

married Kirsten that now just brought him grief because he missed her so much. How they'd had only had a short time together before she'd gotten sick with ovarian cancer. She was like a fleeting shooting star—in and out of his life too quickly.

"You're married," she said gently. "Won't your wife want you home for dinner?"

"No," he said stiffly. "No, I don't have a family, and I don't have a wife."

Pink flushed her cheeks. "I'm sorry. I just assumed..."

"It's okay. I did have a wife, but she's dead. So in answer to your question, no, she won't mind if I work late tonight, Dr. Jensen. In fact, I would prefer to work late and get this surgery up and running before these patients run out of time."

Because he, of all people, knew how keenly time passed before your eyes in a flash.

CHAPTER THREE

VICTORIA TRIED TO concentrate on her work as she went through the files, but it was hard when Matthew was sitting across the table from her and she was still processing his revelation that he was a widower.

She felt bad for him.

At first she had been jealous that he had moved on, but now she felt guilty and her heart hurt for the loss he'd suffered, because it was evident that he loved his late wife.

Victoria had learned from a very young age that there was only one person she could count on and that was herself, but Matthew was different. She'd known that from the first moment she met him, when they were residents and working toward the coveted spot she had ultimately won.

It had scared her how much she had wanted him. How he'd made her feel in that short time they were together. She had been so afraid of having her heart broken, and it was so much easier to push him away. It had been better that way.

Was it?

Her stomach knotted, and there was that part, that one she kept locked away, that couldn't help but wonder how different her life could've been if she had taken the chance on him rather than her career.

He was a stranger. Though they had been hot and heavy, neither talked too much about personal details. They were competitors, after all.

She shook that thought away.

Victoria glanced back at her work. She'd done the right thing. Love wasn't certain.

Look at Matthew—he was a widower. He'd had his heart broken when his wife died.

She didn't get attached to people for a reason.

There was a time in her life when she did. When she had this dream that the father or paternal grandparents she'd never known would come and get her, give her a home, give her security. But each year that ticked by, she grew more and more disappointed, so it was so much easier to disengage.

At least Matthew had had a family to support him. Parents and a wife.

Her heart ached for him to have lost someone he clearly loved.

As if sensing that she was watching him, he glanced up from the file he was working on and cocked an eyebrow.

"Is something wrong?" he asked.

Warmth crept up her neck, and she cleared her throat, tearing her gaze away. "Nothing, just a bit jet-lagged."

A quizzical smile spread across his face. "How? We're in the same time zone."

Drat.

"Hey, it's still tiring having to leave behind Manhattan and come to this…to this…"

"Tropical paradise?" he offered, that old glint of amusement in his eyes. The same sparkle that always made her weak in the knees. The one that made her heart skip a beat and her stomach flutter.

"I suppose." And she couldn't help but smile. She was in paradise. She could be hidden here and do what she loved the most.

Work.

"Look, I know it's a lot of work and probably way more disorganized than you're used to."

"Just a bit." She sighed and then straightened her spine. "I can handle this. I can help."

And she could. She was going to prove to all those naysayers that she wasn't a worthless surgeon.

She was still worth something.

This was what she was good at. She could control this portion of the procedures. All she had to do was do what she always did and throw herself into her work and ignore everything else.

Including all the emotions that Matthew was stirring up in her again.

She wasn't here for him.

She was here for herself. Except that realization made her stomach twist. When had she become so selfish? She was a surgeon, not only for job security, but because she wanted to help people. And as she stared at the large pile of patients' charts, she realized that there were so many people here that needed her.

She couldn't help but wonder how long they had been waiting, and she hoped they were all able to withstand the surgeries. Transplant surgery was grueling on the body, and all these patients would be on antirejection medication for the rest of their lives.

Even then, the kidneys wouldn't last forever. There was a lifespan to donated organs, but at least this was their best chance.

Matthew's phone went off, and he picked it up, frowning as he glanced at the screen. Victoria got a sinking feeling in her stomach.

"What is it?" she asked.

"It's one of the patients that we want to be part of the domino surgery. They're in the emergency room and the doctors want me to come. It's not looking good."

"Can I be of help?" She was worried that he would tell her to stay behind with the files.

"Of course. Follow me and we'll go check on Mrs. Van Luven." Matthew reached down and grabbed his coat off the back of his chair.

A sense of relief washed through her as she picked up the patient's chart out of the pile, and she smiled briefly as she followed Matthew out of the room. Matthew was giving her a chance. He didn't have to do that, but he was and she was very grateful. It was like no time had passed between them. Her heart skipped a beat, and tears stung her eyes.

It was nice to have someone who trusted her again.

Don't get attached. You're not staying here.

And she had to keep reminding herself of that, because once the whole thing in Manhattan blew over, once the press forgot her, she could go back to New York. She could go back to her job and her position.

The one that she won and Matthew didn't.

Right now, she didn't feel like such a winner, but she was grateful for him giving her a chance and letting her be hands-on. She was a good surgeon. She wasn't going to let a rare complication and the press tell her otherwise.

Victoria kept up with Matthew as they made their way back through the twisting hallways of Ziese Memorial down to the emergency room. He waved to the emergency room doctors as he entered and made his way over to a trauma pod that was isolated from the other curtained beds.

Because she was vulnerable and on the donor list, they had isolated the patient to keep her from being exposed to whatever else might be in the air. As Victoria walked through the emergency room, she was impressed with the facilities the hospital had, which were comparable to her hospital in Manhattan.

Ziese Memorial was new and surrounded by the paradise of the city of Charlotte Amalie.

She was a bit jealous of Matthew's good

fortune. She had been so focused on New York City, and now, surrounded by this beautiful hospital in the Caribbean, she couldn't remember why.

Matthew put on a mask and Victoria grabbed one, too, from the box before they stepped into the isolation pod.

"Mrs. Van Luven, I thought I told you I didn't want to see you anytime soon," Matthew joked.

The middle-aged woman laughed, her sunken eyes twinkling slightly despite her waxy and jaundiced complexion. "I'm sorry, Dr. Olesen, I really just can't help myself."

Victoria could tell Matthew was smiling by the way his eyes crinkled over the top of his mask.

"I've brought you a world-renowned specialist."

Mrs. Van Luven's gaze rested on Victoria, and she smiled. "Have you?"

"This is the Dr. Jensen from New York City. She's a transplant surgeon. One of the best."

A blush heated her cheeks, and she was glad that the mask was hiding her reaction to Matthew's compliment.

"It's a pleasure to meet you, Mrs. Van Luven," Victoria said.

"Are you going to help get this domino up and off the ground?" Mrs. Van Luven asked hopefully. "I've been waiting for some time, and I'm too sick to leave the island."

"I plan to," Victoria said, nodding.

"Oh, good." Mrs. Van Luven closed her eyes and relaxed against the pillow, obviously tired.

"What brought her in here today?" Matthew asked the emergency room doctor.

"She was having her regular dialysis, and the dialysis department sent her here, as she's not eliminating enough waste and her numbers are up." The ER doctor handed Matthew a tablet that displayed all the tests they had run, both at the hospital's dialysis center and in the emergency room.

Victoria leaned over Matthew's shoulder to glance at the information.

She frowned, seeing the numbers from the patient's blood work. The dialysis wasn't working, and Mrs. Van Luven was heading toward kidney failure.

This was a difficult case.

"How does it look?" Mrs. Van Luven asked weakly, not opening her eyes.

Matthew and Victoria shared a glance, one that she knew well, and even though she'd done this countless times with other patients, it still felt like there was a rock in the pit of her stomach.

"I think we're going to admit you, Mrs. Van Luven," Matthew said, handing the tablet back to the emergency room doctor.

"Is that necessary?" Mrs. Van Luven asked sadly.

"I'm afraid so. You'll have to stay here while you wait for your transplant," Matthew said gently.

"You mean until I get a transplant…or die," Mrs. Van Luven said softly.

"It's so we can monitor you and provide you the medicines you need," Victoria stated. "That way, I don't have to keep calling you in here all the time to get the cross-match tests I need while I set up the surgery."

It wasn't a lie, but Mrs. Van Luven didn't need to be told that her kidneys were failing, that she was dying. Victoria was a firm believer in the power of the patient's will to live. It wasn't always a sure thing, but it couldn't hurt. Patients needed to know they had a chance.

And as she said that, there was a spark in Mrs. Van Luven's eyes. As if she understood. It gave the patient a glimmer of what Victoria found was sometimes the most potent medicine in the world—hope.

Matthew couldn't help but smile as Victoria gave Mrs. Van Luven that dose of hope, because the numbers that he saw from her tests weren't very encouraging, and he was worried.

Mrs. Van Luven was a forty-three-year-old woman in acute kidney failure.

Matthew knew she had two teenage children and a loving husband at home.

She was too young to die, but then again, so had his wife, Kirsten, been.

And it was the part of the job that he hated the most, losing someone.

Death.

It made him feel like a failure.

Matthew shook that niggling voice away. Victoria had come in and given the patient hope by not promising anything more than stellar hospital care, which was what they provided at Ziese Memorial, but he couldn't form the words, and it hit him hard.

When was the last time he had felt hope?

When had he become so jaded and maudlin?

He wasn't sure, but what Victoria had said

to their patient had worked—there was a little twinkle back in her eyes as Victoria gave instructions to the emergency room doctor about admitting Mrs. Van Luven. He smiled as he watched Victoria. He'd forgotten how smart she was. How good she was with patients. She had never thought she was, but she was wrong.

Victoria always tried to come off as cold and detached, like she didn't need anyone. Except he knew the real her. The compassionate, caring surgeon she tried so hard to hide.

That was the woman he had fallen for.

It's also the woman who'd broken his heart.

"Dr. Tremblay will admit you and I will check on you later. Where is your husband, Rick?" Matthew asked.

"At work," Mrs. Van Luven said. "He wasn't going to leave me, but I thought I'd be okay today. He'll be devastated to know I'm here alone."

Matthew knew that feeling all too well. He sympathized with Rick. "I'll personally call Rick and let him know what's going on."

Mrs. Van Luven nodded. "Thank you, Dr. Olesen and Dr. Jensen."

"You're welcome. I'll be running some labs on your cross matches soon. Try to rest," Victoria added as they left the emergency room pod and closed the glass sliding door behind them. Victoria pulled off her mask, disposed of it and sanitized her hands.

Matthew did the same. "You were great in there."

"How so? I just did my job."

"Yeah, but when you were a resident, I remember you saying you didn't have the best bedside manner. Only you did and you still do."

Victoria snorted, and he knew she didn't believe him. She could never take a compliment. "I still don't. It's one of the chief complaints I seem to get in New York."

"You were great in there. You gave her hope."

Pink tinged her cheeks, and she cleared her throat. "You have the better bedside manner."

"Hardly," he groused.

"You do. I always envied it."

He didn't know what she was talking about. His twin was far more charming than he was.

Matthew rolled his eyes. "Oh, come on, can't you accept a compliment? I mean, I know that you like to be all aloof and cold and detached from patients, but you're anything but."

Her eyes narrowed, and she crossed her arms. "When have I ever said that I like to be detached from my patients?"

"Ten years ago, when I met you," Matthew stated.

And he remembered that day clearly. The first time he'd laid eyes on her, he was immediately attracted to her, but then she'd opened her mouth and he was kind of annoyed at her for a long time.

She always tried to come off as cool and matter-of-fact, but he could see through her facade and knew she actually did care. It was grating on his nerves a bit that she was still denying her gentler side. Like she was afraid of it.

There was nothing wrong with having a gentler side.

A vulnerable side.

And he was keenly aware of that side of her.

"Well," she said, clearing her throat again. "Perhaps, but I don't think I'm much of an ace at it."

"At least you're admitting that you do care about your patients. When I first met you, you didn't even want to admit that."

"It's complicated," Victoria said. "I do care… I mean… Never mind."

"Never mind?" he asked.

What was she hiding? Why did she always have to be so closed off? She hadn't changed.

Did you expect her to?

She rolled her eyes and then blushed again. "Do we really have to do this right now?"

"Why not?"

"Uh, because we're standing in a busy emergency room."

"So, you're willing to talk with me. Just not here?" he asked.

Victoria's eyes darkened into that flinty, menacing, "I'm going to kill you" look. She hadn't changed a bit and he knew that he was pushing her buttons, but he couldn't help himself. Even though he shouldn't, he automatically fell into the old habit, even ten years later.

"Fine," she said stiffly between pursed lips.

"So you're willing to talk?"

"Just not here."

"Okay, then how about we have some dinner tonight and talk? You know, like the good old days. A working dinner while we plan the surgery."

It shocked him that he'd asked her out to

dinner. That hadn't been his intention, but it had just slipped out, and to be honest, it wouldn't be bad to have dinner with someone. Usually his dinners were lonely and sad. He hated them, but it was his reality. He'd loved and lost, twice, and he had no plans to risk his heart again.

A working dinner would be a nice distraction.

Her eyes widened. "What?"

"Dinner. We can have a working dinner." He reiterated it was a working dinner, because that's what it was. It couldn't be anything else.

He wouldn't let it.

Who are you fooling?

He ignored that niggling thought in his head.

"Okay," she said, almost numbly. "Where? I'm not completely familiar with the island…"

"I know a place. I'll take you there. It's not far from the hospital."

"Okay." She nodded again. "Sure."

What am I doing?

Matthew wasn't sure what was coming over him. He didn't want to wallow, and he didn't want her to feel sympathy for him. He didn't want any of that. He was tired of everyone thinking of him as poor widowed Matthew. Even his twin brother, who usually held barely contained annoyance for him on the best of days, sometimes gave him that empathetic doe-eyed look that drove him crazy.

It had been five years since Kirsten had died. It still hurt, but he didn't want sympathy. He wanted to be known for more than being a widower. He wanted to be Matthew again, even if he wasn't sure how to be that person.

So he didn't want that from her.

Not Victoria.

Not the woman who broke his heart.

Then why are you going out to dinner with her?

All he could think was that he was taking her out to dinner because he felt sorry for her. Her career was on hold. His wasn't. She was in hiding, and he wasn't hiding from anything.

Aren't you?

"So, shall we meet in the lobby, then?" Victoria asked, breaking the awkward silence that had fallen between them.

"Yes."

"Okay. I should get back to running labs and the patient profiles."

"Do you need me to take you back the conference room?"

Victoria looked away, tucking a strand of chestnut hair that had come loose from her bun behind her ear. The bun he'd always hated. He much preferred her hair down, but he also liked to see the slender curve of her neck. And he recalled vividly the way she responded when he kissed her there.

What're you doing?

"No. It's fine. I'll meet you in the lobby at seven."

He rubbed the back of his neck awkwardly, trying to shake the memory of kissing her from his mind.

"Okay. Sounds good."

Victoria nodded and left. Matthew watched her walk away. He couldn't tear his gaze from her and her curves. He cursed under his breath as he ran his hand through his hair, completely frustrated with himself. Even after all this time, he was still drawn to her.

Still wanted her.

Dinner with her was a bad idea.

He turned to walk away and ran smack dab

into someone, because he wasn't paying attention and was just trying to get away.

"Sorry," he mumbled, trying to right himself.

"You never usually apologize to me. Though you should on a regular basis," the person quipped.

Matthew groaned.

His twin brother was not the person he wanted to see right now. Hadn't he been tortured enough today?

"I thought you didn't like coming to my island?" Matthew asked dryly.

"I don't. I much prefer St. John, but since you won't answer my calls..."

Matthew sighed. "I'm not ignoring you. I've been busy."

Marcus crossed his arms and cocked an eyebrow. "Really? That's not your usual modus operandi."

"What're you talking about?" Matthew asked.

"You usually ignore me, but my patient—"

"You don't call me socially, either," Matthew said.

"I get busy," Marcus said. "I go out and meet with friends. You just work."

"Work is important."

"So is having a life."

"We were waiting on the organizing surgeon to arrive," Matthew stated. "Give me a break, Marcus. I'm trying my best."

Marcus's eyes narrowed. "My patient is dying, Matthew."

Matthew felt that pang of empathy. He could hear the pain in his brother's voice, and he was very familiar with that tone of desperation.

"I know, and we have a surgeon who is very familiar with dominoes. She just came in from New York."

Marcus raised his eyebrows, impressed. "From New York? How did you manage that? You know what, it doesn't matter. That's great news!"

"Now, will you get off my case?"

Marcus grinned. "We'll see."

Marcus pushed past him, and Matthew shook his head. "Where are you going now?"

"To plead my case with your new surgeon."

Matthew rolled his eyes and watched Marcus leave. He missed his brother sometimes, but today he was stretched to his limit, and Matthew was glad Marcus was out of his hair.

He headed back to this office and sat down in his chair. Bone tired, he leaned back, closing his eyes, before it hit him that Victoria didn't know he had a twin brother. When he and Victoria had been together, they were either in bed or talking work.

Nothing more.

Except that the nothing more had led to love.

He'd lost his heart to Victoria.

And the last thing he wanted was Marcus to know anything about his love life.

You were friends once.

When they had been young, they had been inseparable. Matthew would get so frustrated that Marcus just didn't seem to care about anything and their parents catered to his every whim.

He missed the friendship that they'd had before hormones and teen angst had taken over.

And even if they were close, Matthew wouldn't want anyone to know about his past with Victoria or how she'd broken his heart. He got up. He had to try to stop them from meeting before something bad happened.

Victoria was still stunned she'd agreed to go to dinner with Matthew. That was not what she was here for.

You've got to eat, though, right?

She did, but she was more than capable of eating alone.

In fact, she preferred it.

Who are you kidding?

So maybe she didn't really like eating alone, but was having dinner with Matthew a bad idea? It probably would be fine. Except it hadn't been fine that first time ten years ago, when she'd thought it would be okay to get together with a competitor and had ended up falling into bed with him. She'd gotten lost in his blue eyes, and just thinking back to that moment made her blood heat. And all she wanted to do was kiss him again.

She craved his touch.

Over the years she'd longed to melt in his arms again.

So this dinner was a bad idea. It wouldn't be fine.

Far from it.

But how would it look if she backed out now? She would look like a big old chicken if she did that. What she had to focus on was that it was a working dinner.

Nothing more.

Just two colleagues discussing business. They'd done it hundreds of times in the past. Of course, those talks had almost always ended with them in bed… Heat rushed through her, and she touched her cheeks, suddenly feeling quite flustered. She had to get control of herself.

There was a knock at the door, and she tried to regain her composure.

"Yes?" she called out, her voice shaking slightly.

She turned and saw Matthew standing in the door—or rather, leaning against the doorjamb and gazing at her appreciatively.

Speak of the devil.

"Dr. Olesen, how can I help you?" she asked. Keeping it formal would help her keep her distance.

There was a small moment of surprise, but then his gaze roved over her hungrily, and it sent a shiver of anticipation down her spine. She recalled vividly the last time he'd looked at her like that and what had happened.

The many heated nights they had spent together, wrapped up in each other's arms. The only times in her life she didn't want a romantic moment with someone to end. The only time she had felt safe in someone's arms and hadn't wanted him to leave.

It had scared her. It was hard to breathe when he looked at her like that.

Her stomach did a flip and her skin broke out in gooseflesh, her blood heating. She hated that her body, after all this time, still reacted this way.

"I came to talk to you about the surgery," he said.

"Right. Well, I'm still figuring out the plan. Perhaps we can talk more at dinner?"

He smiled at her. A sly smile, his blue eyes twinkling with a dark promise, one she had seen many times before. "That sounds great."

Now she was confused, because he sounded like he'd forgotten about the dinner he'd just suggested less than half an hour ago. Something seemed a bit off.

"You're the one who suggested it," she said.

"I don't recall doing that," he said, coming toward her.

"What're you talking about?" she asked, annoyed.

"Dinner." And he took a step closer. "What time?"

"Seven." She crossed her arms as he moved closer, as if her arms could be some kind of protective barrier.

"That sounds divine. Where were you thinking?" he asked.

"I don't understand. You said you had a place in mind."

"Actually, I don't."

"Are you being purposefully annoying?" she asked.

"He is." A terse voice came from the door. Her eyes widened as she stared at Matthew standing in the door…while also standing in front of her.

"Matthew," the Matthew who was standing in front of her acknowledged.

"Marcus," the Matthew from the door responded.

"What is going on?" Victoria asked, annoyed.

"Dr. Jensen, meet my identical twin brother, Dr. Marcus Olesen. Marcus, Dr. Jensen is our transplant surgeon, and she's off-limits."

CHAPTER FOUR

"You have a twin?" Victoria asked after Marcus had left and she got over her embarrassment at thinking that Matthew had been coming on to her and how she'd reacted. Now, as she thought about it, she could see the difference between Matthew and his twin.

They were fairly identical, but she felt foolish for not seeing the differences right away.

It was in the eyes. Although they both had blue eyes, Matthew's made her heart beat faster. When he gazed at her, she went weak in the knees. Marcus didn't have that same spark that gave her a secret thrill.

"Yes." Matthew sighed in exasperation.

"You never told me you had a brother, let alone an identical twin."

Matthew shrugged. "Why would I? You were never really interested in learning anything about me. It was just sex and work with you, wasn't it?"

It was like a sucker punch. Their relationship hadn't had a lot of talk for a reason. She didn't want him to get close so she could protect herself from being hurt. When she was with Matthew, she kept it strictly about work. Although, in hindsight, she had longed for more. She just hadn't known how to get it.

She couldn't connect.

It was easier that way. She wouldn't get hurt when it ended and they parted ways. Even if she didn't want to.

You're so afraid that no one will ever be able to love you.

Victoria shook that thought away. That secret fear she tried to keep buried deep down inside her.

"It's not like you tried to get to know me, either," she replied.

A small smile tugged at the corner of his mouth. "Touché."

"Well, I can see the difference now," she mumbled.

Matthew cocked an eyebrow. "Oh, really? How?"

"Well, his hair is slightly longer, and he's more charming. Less rigid," she teased.

Matthew crossed his arms. “What?”

“I’m joking. Well, I guess I’ll have to be more careful in my interactions around here. Don’t want to confuse the two of you.”

“Marcus doesn’t work here. He’s a general practitioner and works on the island of St. John.”

“So you two live on separate islands?” she asked.

“Yes. It’s better that way,” Matthew said firmly.

Victoria cocked an eyebrow. “Really? I would think as twins you two would be really close.”

“A common misconception.”

“It’s not a misconception. Twins are close.”

“Usually,” Matthew stated gruffly. “Not me and my brother, though. I wish at times we were, but it’s always been a competition with him. We’re like night and day. Although there are admirable things about him. Such as his bedside manner. His patients like him more.”

“I’ve told you, you have a great bedside manner,” Victoria said.

Matthew snorted. “As you have said, he’s less rigid.”

“Maybe, but you’re just as good as him.”

"Sure."

"Have you ever told him you want a relationship?" she asked.

Matthew rolled his eyes, clearly annoyed with her. "You're a surgeon, not a therapist. I don't wish to discuss Marcus further."

Victoria understood. There were things she didn't discuss with anyone, either, like her past.

Her lonely, sad, traumatic childhood. Her mother dying when she was ten and her time in foster care.

A shudder traveled down her spine, and for one brief second, she felt that sad pain from when she was a little girl, sleeping on a threadbare mattress, alone in the dark. And all she'd craved was comfort.

Touch.

Victoria wouldn't let herself think about that. She cleared her throat to collect herself. "As a transplant surgeon, I have to make sure my patients are mentally ready for their surgery. There can't be any doubt," she said. "So I guess there's a bit of therapy involved in ascertaining that."

"I'm aware."

She could tell from his serious tone that the discussion was closed.

"So your brother has a patient that needs this surgery?" Victoria asked. "They're on the list, I assume?"

Matthew nodded. "And he's been hounding me since I became chief of surgery to deal with the domino procedure. Not that I blame him."

Victoria sat back down. "And that's what I'm doing. It'll get done."

He smiled, relieved. "I know you will."

Her heart fluttered again at his belief in her. It meant a lot. Especially after what had happened in New York.

There was a knock at the door as a young doctor appeared in the doorway.

"Dr. Jensen?" the young man asked her.

"Yes."

"I'm Dr. Gainsbourg, and I have Mrs. Van Luven's new numbers."

Victoria took the report and went through it. It didn't look good. Her heart sank. "And what kind of dialysis is Mrs. Van Luven currently on?"

"Hemodialysis," Dr. Gainsbourg answered.

Hemodialysis cleaned the blood, but it was clearly no longer working for Mrs. Van Luven. She needed to have abdominal dialysis, which meant surgery.

"We need to get her into surgery so I can place the tube and she has time to heal before we start peritoneal dialysis. Ready Mrs. Van Luven for a surgical procedure once she's done her hemodialysis."

Dr. Gainsbourg nodded. "Of course, Dr. Jensen."

Dr. Gainsbourg left, and she noticed Matthew was staring at her.

"What?" she asked.

"You don't have surgical privileges yet," Matthew stated.

"You had me examine her in your emergency room."

"I know, but I'm more than capable of prepping her for surgery."

"Okay then. By all means, do that. I just want to help, Matthew. I want to do my job."

Matthew's lips pursed together in a thin line. "Fine. You have privileges, obviously, but try to defer to me next time when dealing with my residents."

"Do all your surgeons defer to you? Seems inefficient."

"No," Matthew admitted.

"Then why do I have to?"

"I know my other surgeons. I don't know

you. And I'm in charge of the surgical education program here."

For one moment she'd thought he was trusting her. She'd thought she could do her job effectively here.

Apparently, she'd been wrong.

Victoria clenched her fists and tried to calm her annoyance. "You do know me."

"No. I don't, Victoria. Not really." And with that last comment, he left.

She sat back down, frustrated.

He was right, of course. They didn't know each other. Not anymore. And not really ever. Ten years ago they had had hot, steamy sex and worked well together. She'd fallen in love with him and he with her, but they didn't really know each other. She hadn't known he had a twin and he didn't know about her childhood. They were a force to be reckoned with in the hospital, but that was it.

In every other way, they were strangers.

Strangers who once upon a time had seen each other naked.

Nothing more.

She was here to work, and she was grateful for the opportunity.

Matthew was her boss, and she had to tread carefully.

* * *

Matthew knew he'd been a bit of an ass there, but he didn't trust Victoria. When she'd shown up, he'd planned to keep his distance from her. Only that wasn't working very well. He was falling into the same old routines. He couldn't stop thinking about her, and he hated how panicked and vulnerable he'd felt when he'd realized Marcus had gone up to see her. And when he saw how Marcus looked at her, he'd lost his mind.

He was glad that Marcus hadn't stuck around and found out about his past with Victoria. That was something he didn't want to explain to his nosy brother.

And then it flashed in his mind again—the way his brother had looked at Victoria, like she was some kind of tasty morsel.

Hungrily.

And all he felt was possessive.

And angry.

Don't think about it.

It was done and over with. It was clear that Victoria was not interested in Marcus. Hopefully those two would not run into each other again. Marcus was placated that the domino was on the move again. Patients and potential donors had been notified about testing, which would start in a couple of days, and Matthew was about to go into surgery with Victoria on a simple procedure to keep Mrs. Van Luven stable.

Matthew took a deep, calming breath and headed into the scrub room, where Victoria stood washing her hands. She barely glanced at him, but he could tell she was annoyed. He might say they were strangers, but he did know when he'd ticked her off.

"Dr. Olesen," she grudgingly acknowledged.

"Dr. Jensen."

"Are you going to grill me on my surgical technique?"

"No."

"Oh, really? I figured you would, since you don't know me and all."

Matthew sighed. "I'm sorry for what I said."

"You're so freaking hot and cold you're driving me crazy!" she stated. "I don't remember you being this annoying when we were residents."

At first he thought she was mad, but then he saw the twinkle in her eyes.

She was teasing him.

He chuckled softly, leaned over and whispered, "I was, but you were blinded by my sexual prowess."

Then he froze, not sure what had come over him. He had teased her the way he used to. For one moment he'd forgotten ten years had passed, and he hoped he hadn't offended her or made her feel uncomfortable.

Victoria snorted. "Right."

He breathed a sigh of relief.

Just like old times.

"I'm sorry," he said, scrubbing under the water. "There's been a lot going on."

"You're preaching to the choir," she ruminated. "Can we just work together and be professional? Now I know you have a doppelgänger on the other island, I'll avoid St. John and him."

"Thank you. It's a shame, though, as St. John is a beautiful island, too."

"If only it didn't have your brother?" she teased.

He smiled. "Precisely."

"Well, I don't understand sibling relationships, as I don't have any, but consider it noted."

There was a bit of sadness in her voice, and he couldn't picture being sad about being an only child. There were many times he'd wished he was an only child himself.

No, you don't.

An image of Marcus and him in their goofy tree house on St. Croix flitted through his mind. They had been ten at the time. Before they had been shipped off to boarding school.

Before Matthew had taken on the role of parenting Marcus.

When they'd still been friends.

He smiled to himself as he remembered it clearly. The joy, the happiness and the fun. It had been some time since he'd thought of that ramshackle tree house.

Victoria finished scrubbing and headed into the operating room, where they were finishing the prep on Mrs. Van Luven.

Matthew finished and followed her as the nurses helped him put on a surgical gown.

Mrs. Van Luven was visibly shaking. The operating room was usually colder than the rest of the hospital, but that wasn't why his patient was shaking.

She was terrified.

And he couldn't blame her.

Matthew made his way over to her.

"How are you?" he asked, gently.

"Nervous," Mrs. Van Luven said, her voice quivering.

"Don't be. Dr. Jensen knows what she's doing, and this is a standard, straightforward procedure." Though Victoria was just assisting him, he wanted to ensure his patient had complete trust in Victoria's skills, because he did.

Mrs. Van Luven smiled, but it was still wobbly. "Okay."

Matthew headed back over to Victoria, who was waiting as the anesthesiologist worked to put the patient asleep.

"The patient is under," the anesthesiologist said a few moments later.

"Why don't you take the lead, Dr. Jensen?" Matthew offered.

Victoria's eyebrows raised. "Are you sure?"

"Positive. Let's see what you can do after all this time."

Victoria nodded and began the procedure. Matthew didn't know why he was here. Victoria didn't need him. She was so talented. The press was crazy for questioning her, and the hospital in New York was crazy for forcing her to take a break.

Although he was thankful they had, as it meant she was here and he could watch her work. He'd forgotten how much he enjoyed working with her.

How much he admired her.

"You okay?" Victoria asked, looking up from her work.

"Fine. Why?" he asked.

"I thought you were going to assist, since you handed me the lead."

"Do you need me to?"

"Not really."

"I'm here to observe and assist if needed." As he stood back to watch her work, an alarm went off, and a sense of dread traveled down his spine.

"Dammit," Victoria cursed under her breath.

"What's wrong?"

"I'm pretty sure there's a clot," Victoria murmured, panic lacing in her voice.

"Okay," Matthew said calmly. "We can deal with that."

He stepped forward and helped her as he glanced at the patient's vitals.

"Sats are dropping," the anesthesiologist announced.

Victoria was frozen, her eyes wide, as if she didn't know what to do. He'd been teaching residents for a year or so, and he knew that look of fear.

"Hey," he said gently.

Victoria looked at him, terror in her eyes, which was so unlike the Victoria he knew.

"We can deal with this, Victoria. What do we do?"

"Evacuate the clot."

"Right. You know what to do next," he said.

Victoria nodded and got back to work, as if that blip hadn't happened. It was only a moment that she'd frozen, unsure of herself.

It was a side of her he'd never seen before. Not that he could blame her for feeling this way after New York. And in that moment he wanted to hold her. She was capable, but her confidence had been shaken.

"Push some epinephrine," Victoria barked over her shoulder, pulling out the laparoscopic instruments and opening the incision wider.

Matthew tuned out all the flurry of activity and focused on the patient. Now was not the time to get panicked.

The only time he'd let the wearing sound of the monitor get to him was when Kirsten had been slipping away and he'd had to watch her leave him.

And then there it was. The bleeding and the clot.

"Do you see it?" he asked.

Victoria glanced up. "Yes. Suction."

Matthew nodded as Victoria cleaned up the source of the problem. The moment the clot was evacuated, Mrs. Van Luven's vitals returned to normal. Victoria breathed a sigh of relief and continued with the procedure.

Matthew stepped away. "I'll let you finish up, Dr. Jensen. Excellent work."

"Thanks." Her voice shook as she spoke. "And thank you for your help. I don't know what came over me."

He smiled behind his mask. "You're welcome."

He turned and left the operating room, disposing of his gown, gloves and mask.

As he scrubbed out, he took another deep breath. For one moment he'd thought he was back there with Kirsten as she died, and he hated that that thought had crept in.

There were times he had become almost paralyzed with fear just after Kirsten first died, but there had been no one to talk him out of his trance.

He'd had to work it out himself.

He didn't like sharing that with anyone, but he was glad that he'd been able to help Victoria at that moment. He was glad to be there for her, and that thought scared him.

He needed to keep a firm grasp on his emotions, and he was annoyed at how fast he'd lost control around Victoria.

CHAPTER FIVE

SOMETHING STRANGE HAD come over Matthew during that surgery, and Victoria wasn't sure what it was.

Then the clot had struck, and she'd frozen.

All she could hear was the flat-line monitor from New York in her head. Then she'd seen Matthew, and she'd remembered what to do. He'd gotten through to her, and it scared her that he had. She'd been vulnerable and exposed, and he'd talked her down. He calmed her and she was glad he was there, but it scared her how she had relied on him in that moment.

Victoria was certainly questioning her sanity as she made her way down to the main lobby of Ziese Memorial Hospital for her dinner date with Matthew. There was part of her that hoped he wouldn't be there waiting for her so she could head back to the small apartment she'd rented for the month and have an easy night instead.

Yeah, that's what you need. Time alone with your thoughts.

Victoria shook that thought away as she entered the main lobby and spotted Matthew standing by the doors. He looked so different out of his scrubs and white jacket. He was dressed in jeans, a blue button-down shirt that brought out his blue eyes and a brown suit jacket. It was business casual, and her heart skipped a beat.

When they had been residents, he had never dressed as tailored or professional, but then, they had been still learning and really didn't have time to worry about their images. Most of their time was spent at the hospital.

Her stomach did that flip again, and she recalled the way he used to look at her with those blue eyes that always held a promise of something more. Something that made her weak in the knees. He didn't look at her the same way anymore, and that was her fault.

Still, she couldn't help but feel nervous as she walked toward him.

At least she hoped it was him. She wouldn't know until she looked into his eyes.

"Matthew?" she asked cautiously.

He turned, and a small smile tugged at the corner of his mouth. "Yes, it's me. I thought you could tell us apart?"

She smiled, relieved. "I just wanted to make sure. Your brother might've gotten his hair cut or something."

He chuckled at that. "He's gone back to St. John, or at least I think he has. He tends to come and go as he pleases."

"Does he have a plane? Because I was led to believe that the ferry schedules are set."

"He lives on a boat," Matthew mumbled.

"He really does rub you the wrong way, doesn't he?" she asked.

"Just a bit." He glanced at his watch. "Are you ready to go?"

"Sure. I'm looking forward to this working dinner."

He looked at her strangely. "Such an emphasis on the *working* part. What do you think is going to happen?"

"Nothing, and that's why I emphasized it," she snapped and then instantly regretted her outburst. Matthew was complaining that Marcus pushed his buttons, but she'd forgotten about all the times that Matthew and she had gotten on each other's nerves when they were residents.

They were either driving each other crazy at work or in each other's arms.

It had been one of the best times of her life. She could have loved him, but she was so scared to reach out and take it. So scared of what love would do to her life, so she'd let it go.

Even though she'd regretted it ever since.

She quickly shook that thought away as she followed Matthew out of the hospital and into the warm, breezy dusk of Charlotte Amalie.

Ziese Memorial was located farther up from the main turquoise waters of the harbor. Charlotte Amalie, the capital of St. Thomas, with its distinctive red rooftops, was built against the lush green volcanic hillside of the island, and as the sun set, the lights of the city were coming on, and she could see the lights of the large cruise ships that were docked in the port.

It was like something out of a travel guide.

She liked the lights sparkling against the darkness, letting her know that there were lives out there.

She wasn't alone.

She wasn't afraid with that comfort.

Matthew stopped in front of a luxury car and opened the door for her.

“This is your car?” she asked, shocked.

“It is. The restaurant is down by the water, and your heels aren’t really made for walking.”

“I’m a New Yorker—we’re used to walking. Even in heels.”

“If I’m not mistaken, by my memory, New York City is fairly flat. Charlotte Amalie is hilly. Get in,” he urged gently. “You’ll thank me.”

She slid into the leather passenger seat, and he shut the door. She watched him walk around the front of his car and climb into the driver’s side.

“I hope you like seafood. There is a little bistro down in French Town by Cay Bay that I like to frequent.”

“That sounds good.” She really didn’t care where they went, as long as she could get a glass of wine. “Honestly, I thought you’d take me to Bluebeard’s castle and have me beheaded like the rest of his women.”

Matthew chuckled. “Hardly—well, at least not until you get your work done.”

Victoria laughed. “I will get it done.”

It was nice to laugh and tease with him like they had when they were residents.

She had missed this.

They drove in silence through Charlotte Amalie to French Town. The bistro was located almost on the water's edge in sight of all the luxury yachts that were moored in the harbor. Matthew parked, got out and opened the door for her.

As he locked his car, he muttered under his breath.

"What?" she asked.

"My brother is still here. His boat is moored out there in the Cay."

Victoria's eyes widened as she looked at all the luxury boats that were anchored in the turquoise waters. They weren't the kind of boats that she had been picturing when Matthew had mentioned that his twin lived on a boat.

"I didn't think general practitioners made money like that!"

Matthew shrugged. "They don't. Our parents bought him that boat. Well, technically, it was my father's first boat, but he has something bigger and faster now, and Marcus got the old one."

"Your parents live nearby?"

"They live on St. Croix, where I grew up. It's about a ninety-minute ferry ride from here."

They walked down the cobbled street toward the bistro, which was lively and full of tourists. She was worried they wouldn't be able to get a table, but as soon as Matthew approached the maître d', he was shown right in.

All Victoria could do was follow as they wound their way through the crowded lower restaurant and up some narrow stairs to a beautiful rooftop patio, which was much quieter and cooler.

"Is this suitable, Dr. Olesen?" the maître d' asked.

"Yes. Thank you."

The maître d' smiled and held out Victoria's chair for her. "Your waiter will be with you shortly. In the meantime, would you like some of our house wine?"

"Yes!" Victoria said, a bit too eagerly, which made Matthew chuckle.

The maître d' smiled and nodded. "I'll be back momentarily."

Matthew nodded as the maître d' left them, and then it was just the two of them, under string lights overlooking the water of Charlotte Amalie. In the distance she could hear music playing, and there was a murmur of chatting and laughing below.

"So, if your parents gave your brother a luxury yacht, is the car a gift from them, too?"

"Yes. I've had it for a while. Another one of my father's castoffs. Not that I mind this particular castoff."

"I had no idea your parents were megarich, which they are by the sounds of it."

Matthew shrugged. "Things were not always handed to us. My father reminds us all the time he worked to amass his fortune and made it clear we had to work to live. He doesn't pay our way."

"Fair enough. I wanted to thank you for your help in the surgery today."

A strange expression crossed his face, his lips pursed together. "Why? I didn't do much."

"You calmed the patient down, and you were my second set of eyes when we were looking for that clot. I'm glad you were there."

"No, you're not."

Victoria rolled her eyes. "Are you going to argue with everything Io say?"

"No," he said softly. "I'm sorry. I guess I'm really not used to you complimenting anyone, because you certainly didn't when we were residents. You were sort of a force to be reckoned with."

"Were?"

They smiled, and that twinkle in his eyes, the one that she was so familiar with, was back, and it made her heart skip a beat.

The maître d' returned with the wine and poured them both a glass.

"Here's to a successful domino?" Matthew asked, raising his glass.

She raised her glass to meet his. "There is no question. This will go off well."

They both took a sip, and it was exactly what she needed after such a trying day. Victoria was completely wrung out.

"I know it will," he stated, setting his glass down. "And I know you'll quickly get a handle on it. I'm annoyed that my predecessor let it sit for as long as he did, and I'm glad you were able to come and help."

"I didn't really have a choice, if you remember," she said, clearing her throat and trying not to think of the nightmare that had brought her to this tropical paradise. She missed Manhattan and her life there.

Or, at the very least, she missed her work life there.

She really didn't have much of a social life. There was no time, given that she devoted every ounce of herself to her work.

Her gaze roved over the yachts that were gently bobbing in the water below them. "So which one is Marcus's?"

"Why? Are you interested in my twin?"

She shot him a withering glance. "One of you is enough, but you have me curious. You said your father gave it to Marcus because he upgraded, and I'm having a hard time picturing what he upgraded to."

Matthew chuckled softly. "The one closest to the shore. It's slightly smaller. It's called *Tryphine*."

She cocked her eyebrow. "That's an unusual name."

"Well, it's related to the Bluebeard myth."

"I don't know much about that. I was only remarking on it because of the Bluebeard's castle historic site. So, tell me about Tryphine."

"St. Tryphine," Matthew corrected. "She is the patron saint of sick children and overdue mothers. She is thought to be the basis for the Bluebeard fable. She was from Breton and married an awful man named Conomor to stop him from invading her father's lands. When he was away, she found the bodies of his deceased wives, and as she prayed over them, they warned her that Conomor would kill her if she became pregnant."

"And she was pregnant?"

Matthew nodded. "It had been speculated that his child would kill him, so he would kill his wives when they were pregnant so that none of his children survived. The deceased wives tried to help Tryphine escape, and she did. She gave birth to their son, but soon Conomor found her and cut off her head."

Victoria winced. "A lovely thing to name a boat after."

"It has a happy ending. St. Gildas found her and restored her life. Meanwhile, there's debate about whether it was Tryphine's son that actually ended up killing his father, or the castle itself, as some say after he beheaded Tryphine, he went back to his castle and the castle crumbled on top of him. The moral is that Tryphine protects pregnant mothers and sick children, and my brother deals a lot with pregnant women and sick children. It's his passion, so when he got the boat, he changed the name from *Freja*—our mother's name—to *Tryphine*. It's one thing I actually think he got right. My late wife thought so, too."

And then she saw his spine stiffen.

She wanted to ask him what his wife had

been like, but suddenly the waiter appeared with their menus and was rattling off the specials. Victoria couldn't focus. All she could think about was how much it clearly pained Matthew to talk about his late wife, and she wondered how long it had been since his wife had passed. The waiter left to give them time to decide what they wanted.

She tried to figure out what she wanted to eat but couldn't make up her mind. "Any suggestions?"

Matthew glanced up. "To eat?"

"Yes. How about you order for the both of us? I'm not picky. You do it and get me something that St. Thomas is well-known for."

"You're putting a lot of trust in me," he remarked.

"Shouldn't I?" she asked.

He grinned and winked. "Okay, then I think we should have conch and fungi."

"Conch and what?" she asked.

"Fungi. It's like a polenta—it's lovely and I think you'll enjoy it."

"Okay. I like the sound of that."

The waiter came back, and she let Matthew order for them.

"So, when do the people come in for the cross-match tests?" he asked.

"They start coming in tomorrow. The sooner we get this done and I can refer them to counseling, the better. We have six potential recipients, and I need six donors."

"And if we don't have enough donors?"

"That's what I'm worried about. Mrs. Van Luven is incredibly unstable. She needs peritoneal dialysis, and it should've been done long before this. Hemodialysis has been failing her for some time."

Matthew nodded. "I know. Her physician was the former chief."

"Well, the tubing is in now, at least, but she needs to heal. So we're going to have to keep her hooked up for hemodialysis and keep trying to keep her stable. I need her stronger for the transplant."

"She's young and a mother..." He trailed off.

"How long ago did your wife die?" she asked gently.

The question caught him off guard, but as he thought of Mrs. Van Luven dying, knowing that she had children, he couldn't help but think of Kirsten and the cancer that took her life. They had wanted kids, but when she couldn't get pregnant and had irregular bleeding, she'd gone to see her doctor.

It was then they had found the unimaginable—cervical and ovarian cancer that had spread.

Marcus had named the boat *Tryphine* because Kirsten wanted him to name it that. Marcus adored Kirsten, and it was something small that took her mind off the cancer treatments.

Marcus and Kirsten's friendship gave her pleasure, and for a brief period of time Matthew was glad to have Marcus there, and Marcus actually wanted to be around him. A time when they had pulled together to support Kirsten…

"What shall I call it? I really don't want a boat named after my mother," Marcus stated.

Matthew rolled his eyes. "There's nothing wrong with Freja*."*

Kirsten scolded him. "Don't be so mean to your brother. He's absolutely right that this is his vessel now and he needs to choose a name he likes."

"Don't you like my mother?" he teased.

"You know that I do," Kirsten said sweetly.

"Still, a single man shouldn't have a boat named after his mother."

Marcus stuck his tongue out at Matthew and then laughed.

"Don't be childish, Marcus," Matthew groused, trying not to laugh as well.

"Don't be such a stick in the mud, Matthew," Marcus snapped back. "Kirsten, since you're always kind and sweet to me, I want you to name her."

Kirsten smiled. "How about Tryphine*?"*

"What?" Matthew asked, confused.

"The patron saint of sick children, I believe," Marcus said.

"And of overdue mothers," Kirsten said sadly. "Mothers who never got to be mothers..."

Marcus and Matthew shared a look. Marcus knew how much Kirsten wanted a child, and with the cancer that just wasn't possible at the moment.

*"*Tryphine *it is, then!" Marcus announced. "She'll be the only one in the Caribbean, I'm sure."*

Matthew shook the memory away.

He had no problem with his brother's boat, but the memories it brought… He missed those times when Kirsten brought peace between him and Marcus. She was a beautiful light, and he missed her.

Kirsten was always present in the back of his mind since she'd died five years ago, but since Victoria had landed back in his life, his late wife was suddenly front and center in his thoughts again.

When he was with Kirsten, he was haunted by memories of Victoria, and apparently when he was with Victoria, he was haunted by memories of Kirsten. The two times he'd loved, he'd lost, and it still hurt. He never wanted to feel that way again.

Yet Victoria was already getting under his skin. Just like she used to do.

He couldn't let himself fall for her again.

It would hurt too much.

Except it was so hard to keep away from her.

"She died five years ago." he said stiffly, answering the question. He didn't like talking about Kirsten with anyone. Yet here he was talking about her with Victoria. The only other woman who had broken his heart, though in a very different way.

"I'm so sorry," she whispered.

"Thank you, but I'd rather not open up a pity party. She's gone, and when I talk about her, people change around me. Their sympathy…it makes me feel like I'm drowning, trapping me in a never-ending cycle of grief. And though I do grieve for her—I always will—I don't want to wallow in it."

"I understand that."

"Do you?" he asked, because she'd never mentioned her family. The only thing he knew about her was that she was from New York and she didn't have any siblings. When they were together ten years ago, she'd never shared that part of herself.

And he'd never shared his life with her. They had been so wrapped up in each other, they didn't want to let anyone else in to upset the balance.

He reached across the table to touch her but drew his hand back when the waiter brought their food.

"Let me know what you think of it," Matthew said, trying to change the subject after the waiter had gone, hoping she hadn't noticed how he'd tried to reach out and touch her, like the weak fool that he was when he was with her.

"It smells great. I've never had conch before. I've had polenta…"

"Fungi is better, trust me, and for dessert we'll have some johnnycakes."

Victoria took a bite, and he could tell that she approved of his choice. They had come a long way from eating hot dogs from the cart outside the hospital. Thinking about all those times they'd dashed outside on a quick break to get one made him smile.

"What're you smiling about?" she asked.

"I was thinking about how we'd huddle around Jacob's cart. Remembering the steam and the biting cold wind, but those dogs were great."

"Yeah. I miss him."

"Is he no longer there?" Matthew asked.

"He passed on, sadly. A year after you left."

"I'm sorry to hear that."

"Yeah, now I mostly go to that deli—the one we went to when we were tired of hot dogs. That's still there."

"Oh, the delicatessen is still there? That's good to know. I do miss those pastrami sandwiches. You can't really get good pastrami here."

"This is much nicer scenery, though," she said. "And probably a bit better for overall cholesterol levels."

They shared a laugh again.

"So, is your family worried about you being so far away?" Matthew asked.

"Family?" she asked, confused. "I'm not married."

"No, I mean your parents. You mentioned you don't have siblings..."

"No," she said quickly, looking down at her plate. "No. I don't have any family missing me."

"Oh, I'm sorry."

She shrugged indifferently. "It is what it is. I'm just glad that I was offered a chance to escape here and help."

"Is this an escape?" he asked gently.

"Yes," she stated. "I freely admit that I ran here because it was the only place I could come."

"If you'd known that I was here, would you still have come?"

A pink blush crept up her slender neck and bloomed in her cheeks. He was expecting her to say no. He wanted a reaction from her, something to let him know that she was struggling just as much as he was with being back in his life, but instead of Matthew getting her answer, the waiter came back and refilled their wine and took away their plates, letting them know their dessert would be delayed as he discreetly left.

Matthew didn't care about the wine or the dessert, he just wanted an answer. He was so focused on it.

Gentle music played in the background as they sat there in uneasy silence.

It made him agitated and anxious. He couldn't just sit here. He had to do something.

"Come on," he said, standing up and holding out his hand. He didn't know what he was doing. Maybe it was the wine, or this night, or this day in general, but he just couldn't sit here.

"What?" she asked, confused.

"We're going to dance."

She looked at him like he was crazy, but she didn't argue as she slipped her hand in his and stood. He took her in his arms but didn't hold her too close. Matthew was experimenting, and he wanted to see how close he could get to her, but even though he tried to keep her at bay, his body still reacted.

He could remember what it was like to hold her in his arms, to run his hands over her curves and kiss her.

The way her body quivered under his touch.

His blood heated, and his mouth went dry.

She was so close.

"You're an idiot," she murmured, not looking at him.

He laughed. "What do you mean?"

"What possessed you to dance on the rooftop?"

He shrugged. "It's a good song, and it seemed like a perfect night. I felt like dancing. Haven't you ever felt like dancing before?"

She gazed at him, her eyes twinkling. "No. I can't say that I have."

"That's a shame." He spun her around, making her laugh as he spun her back toward him. Only this time, she came closer.

"You asked if I would still have come here knowing that you were chief, and the answer is yes. I would've."

"You would?"

"If you'd asked me to," she whispered, the pink blooming in her cheeks again.

He stared at her lips. Drank in her intoxicating scent and felt her tremble in his arms. Before he knew what he was doing, he stopped the dance and leaned in to kiss her.

To drink in those soft lips.

Her body went limp, and he wrapped his arms around her, pulling her in for a deeper kiss. Drowning himself in her softness. It had been so long since he'd been burned by her kisses and he welcomed the fire.

What're you doing?

Victoria pushed him away, stepping back. "We can't."

"I know," he said. "I'm sorry. I don't know what came over me."

"It's okay, but I think we'd better skip dessert and I'll just go back to my place and you go back to yours. We need to keep this professional."

He nodded. "I'll go pay the bill, and then I'll take you home."

Victoria sat back down, and he headed downstairs.

What had come over him?

He was acting foolishly.

They had to keep this strictly professional. He couldn't get lost in Victoria's kisses again.

He just couldn't.

CHAPTER SIX

MATTHEW HAD BEEN avoiding her for the last week, which was fine by Victoria. After that kiss, she couldn't sleep. It had been wonderful, but also so bad.

So very bad.

There was also a part of her that had missed him this week, even though she knew it was better they keep their distance, because her time here was temporary.

She'd gotten over him once—she could get over him again.

She'd done it before, even though there was a part of her that didn't want to do it again.

It was better this way, though.

Matthew was the most infuriating man she'd ever known, but she'd forgotten what it was like to be with him and how she forgot herself and all the protective barriers she'd set up to protect her heart. Even ten years later, he could get through them. And she didn't know why he'd been the only man to do so.

She'd learned as a child not to trust anyone, that you could only rely on yourself. That's why she kept people at a distance.

But then she'd met Matthew, and she couldn't keep him away. She was lost to him.

She was weak when it came to him, and she didn't like being that powerless.

Not to anyone.

What're you so afraid of?

She ignored that niggling thought, just like she tried to forget about that dance and that kiss they'd shared a week ago.

The only solution was work. That's how she had gotten over him before.

She threw herself into her work and getting the domino surgery up and running. Dr. Gainsbourg had been assigned to her, and she had the young student run all her labs while she vetted potential donors and waited for cross matches to come in.

Each recipient had an incompatible donor or donors, and the only way a recipient who wasn't eligible to donate to the person they cared for would donate was if their person got a kidney in return.

So it took a lot of prep work. It took a lot of labs.

There were a lot of moving pieces to this surgery, and since she didn't have any other regular surgeries planned, she took it on with gusto.

Plus, it kept her distracted and away from Matthew, who was busy with his own surgical practice as well as running the hospital.

It was better this way. No one would get hurt again this way.

Once this domino procedure was over and done with, she was hoping that she would be able to head back to Manhattan, but so far, she hadn't heard a word from Paul or the hospital there. She had to wait until the autopsy cleared her, but she was still disappointed a week had gone by and the press attention hadn't blown over.

Victoria sighed and went back to reading the lab reports, but it was no good. Thinking about New York also reminded her how she had frozen when Mrs. Van Luven threw a clot.

She loathed the uncertainly and the terror she had felt in that moment. She was so sure of her work. Clots had never fazed her before.

If it hadn't been for Matthew... Well, she didn't want to think about it.

It was just better to keep her head down and out of people's way.

In particular, out of Matthew's way.

She had thought it was absolutely absurd when he took her hand and pulled her up to dance—it was like he was trying to tempt fate—but she couldn't deny she'd been thrilled to be in his arms again. The memory of his kiss flashed through her mind, and her cheeks heated. She touched her lips and smiled.

She'd lost herself.

And she didn't know when it had happened.

Victoria set down the report she was reading and got up to stretch her back.

She was antsy and full of nervous energy, so she paced around the room and stared out of the window of Ziese Memorial at all the red-roofed buildings that wound their way over hillsides and down to the turquoise water. There were palm trees blowing in the breeze. She couldn't remember the last time she had seen trees blowing in the wind like this, or when she'd taken the time to just watch them. It was relaxing. There was another large cruise ship making its way into the port, and for one brief moment she wished she could escape.

Just climb aboard the ship and go off somewhere new.

No responsibilities.

Not a care in the world.

Except she loved her job. She was living out her dream, and she wasn't going to stop because of a temporary setback.

There was a knock at the door, and she turned to see Matthew's lookalike, making her heart skip a beat, just for a fraction of a second. At least she could tell them apart now. She felt foolish for not noticing the differences before.

"Dr. Olesen… Marcus. How can I help you?"

Marcus grinned. "So you've figured out how to tell us apart, then?"

"I have." She left the window and motioned for him to come in, which he did, shutting the door behind him. "What brings you here today? Matthew told me you went back to St. John, but then he was grumbling when we saw your boat in the port on the way to dinner."

Marcus paused and raised his eyebrows, in

a quirk so much like his brother. "You were with him at night?"

"Yes, we had a working dinner the day I got you two confused and accidentally suggested you and I were going to dinner."

"Yeah, but I didn't think you'd choose my brother over me. I'm much better dinner company than him. He's too uptight." There was a wide grin that she was positive probably charmed people, but it did nothing for her.

It wasn't the same as Matthew. Matthew's smile made her pulse race.

Marcus might think Matthew was uptight, but Victoria didn't think so. She smiled as she thought about him, about his arms around her as they danced.

Then she remembered Marcus was waiting for her response.

Quick. Think of something to say.

"We were discussing the surgery. A work dinner, as I said. Then he saw your boat."

"Well, I did eventually go back to St. John, but I had some other business I had to attend to, and as it pertains to the surgery, I came back to discuss it with you."

"Oh? And what's there to discuss?"

Marcus handed her the sheet. "It's a lab result, and it solves your problem. I know that the surgery is being delayed because you're having a hard time finding a cross match for Mrs. Van Luven, as no donors in the other incompatible pairs match with her."

It was true.

Mrs. Van Luven was the only one in the domino who didn't yet have a donor, even though she was the one who needed it the most. Victoria was aware that Mrs. Van Luven was also far down the deceased donor list. If she became any more ill, she would move up the list, but there were no guarantees she would still survive the surgery at that point. She glanced at the report and saw the antibodies were a match.

It was almost absolutely perfect.

She smiled. "This is fantastic!"

"Yep, it's a donor who has a mild interest in the operation, as someone they care for is having the surgery."

"Who? What patient?"

"The patient happens to be a fifteen-year-old boy, and that boy happens to be my best friend's kid and my godson."

A sinking feeling knotted her stomach. "Oh, no, Marcus, please don't tell me it's you!"

"And if it is?" Marcus asked.

Victoria sighed. “We can’t take you.”

“Why not?”

“It’s a conflict of interest.”

“How? I’m not a surgeon on this file, and I’m not Mrs. Van Luven’s physician. Jonas is my godson, and his father is like the brother I never had.”

“You have a brother, Marcus. He’s my boss.”

Marcus snorted. “Biologically, but we haven’t been close since we were teens. Everything is a competition with him.”

“Funny. He said the same about you.”

Marcus’s eyes narrowed, and a strange expression crossed his face before he shook his head in frustration. “Look, Jonas means the world to me, and I want to donate my kidney to Mrs. Van Luven so this surgery can take place and Jonas can get his kidney in the domino.”

Victoria glanced at the report. She couldn’t recall if there were any specific rules against this. He was donating it of his own free will, just like all the other donors were. Would it be that much of a problem if he was in the domino? She could do the retrieval herself and have Matthew start on Mrs. Van Luven until she got there.

It was a solution.

Except he was the chief's brother.

She wouldn't want to put Matthew's identical twin in any kind of danger. Marcus sat down backward on a chair across from her, grinning.

"You're thinking about it, aren't you?" Marcus asked.

"Perhaps." She glanced at the report again. "I don't know about this, Marcus. You're Jonas's physician."

"Only because there was no other physician on the island at the time to take care of him, but I'm his godfather first. I always have been. I want to do this. He'll die if this surgery doesn't happen, just like the others."

"I'll have to talk to your brother about this."

"Why?" Marcus asked.

"He's the chief of surgery and your brother."

Marcus rolled his eyes. "I get it, I suppose. Look, I'm not a surgeon, and I don't have hospital privileges here. Here, I'm just someone who wants to do something for the greater good."

She smiled at him, moved by his selflessness. "Fine. I will run it by Matthew, and if he approves, you still need to go through the counseling sessions I've set up."

"Counseling?" he asked.

"Yes. It's mandatory for all donors and recipients." She stood up. "So you're really, really, really sure about this?"

Marcus nodded. "I am."

"Thank you. This might solve our problem."

He grinned a sideways grin that was sort of like Matthew's, only his mouth curled to the opposite side of his twin brother's. "I'm glad I can be a problem solver."

"Stick around. I'm going to go see your brother right now."

"I will."

Victoria left the room, her stomach was twisting in a knot as she walked toward Matthew's office. She knew that he was going to have a problem with it, but that wasn't what was bothering her. She was nervous. Her stomach was doing flip-flops. She hadn't seen him since their kiss, and she couldn't stop thinking about it. She just hoped it wouldn't be weird when they saw each other. Victoria knew Matthew was avoiding her, too.

He'd sent her emails, but that was it.

He hadn't come to personally check on the progress of the domino.

Maybe he has faith in you?

Victoria snorted to herself. She highly doubted that.

She wondered if he regretted the kiss just as much as she did. Except she wasn't really regretting the kiss. Not at all. It shouldn't have happened, but there was a part of her—the one that she had long thought she'd buried deep down inside her—that actually wanted it to continue.

The part of her that wanted to stay with him because she loved him—the only man she had ever loved.

The part of her that wanted to say to hell with the job and take a chance on love, but that had lost out to the rational side of her.

The survivor side of her.

Even if she'd regretted that moment for the last ten years.

And she knew that kiss was a mistake. She wanted to be friends and colleagues with Matthew, but that was all. They couldn't go backward. There was no way to turn back time.

Why not?

Victoria shook that thought away and knocked on Matthew's door.

"Come in."

She opened the door, and he glanced up,

his eyes widening, and he opened his mouth, probably to tell her he was busy or something.

"Yeah, I know you're not busy, and you don't have to fake a phone call or a meeting. This won't take long." She shut the door.

Matthew frowned. "Fine. I've been avoiding you."

"Oh? Have you? I thought I was the one avoiding you," she teased.

He smiled. "What do you need, Victoria?"

"A donor has come forward. One that is an excellent match for Mrs. Van Luven."

"Really?" Matthew asked, and he held out his hand for the report.

"There's a catch," she said, her stomach twisting.

"What's that?" He was scanning over the numbers.

"It's Marcus."

"What?" He set the report down like it was on fire.

"Marcus did a cross match, or had someone do it. Apparently his godson, Jonas, is one of the recipients, and though he wasn't a match for Jonas, he's a match for Mrs. Van Luven. I don't have to explain to you that we're running out of time to find a living donor match for Mrs. Van Luven or even a nonliving organ donor. There are others ahead of her on the list. Ones not compatible for the domino and from other islands. If we wait for her to get sicker to move up the list, I'm worried she won't survive the surgery. She needs to be a part of this domino. It's her only chance."

Matthew leaned back in his chair and scrubbed a hand over his face. "I know."

"I thought it could potentially be a conflict of interest, but he doesn't know Mrs. Van Luven, and he's not a surgeon or a physician here. He's just someone who wants to be a living donor."

"He knows a lot of the surgeons here, though. Who is going to do his surgery?" Matthew asked. He sounded tired or possibly annoyed.

"I will. You can start on Mrs. Van Luven while I retrieve Marcus's kidney, and then I can continue with Mrs. Van Luven's procedure."

"While also overseeing the others?" Matthew asked in disbelief.

"I have done this before," she reminded him.

"Dammit, Marcus," Matthew cursed under his breath.

"I get the feeling you think of him as the

evil twin and you think of yourself as the good twin. I also think he thinks the opposite."

"Of course he does," he mumbled. "Because he's the evil twin. Besides, that's cliché of you."

"Well, what am I to think? You hate him so much."

"I don't hate him," Matthew said tiredly. "I just hate how he always tries to one-up me."

"I think this has more to do with his godson."

Matthew's expression softened. "Of course. I guess I can't fault him for that."

"If you do, you're clearly the evil twin," she teased.

Matthew chuckled. "Fine."

Victoria smiled. "Are we good to go with this surgery?"

"Did he agree to getting the counseling?"

Victoria nodded. "Yes. I told him I wouldn't accept him unless he did the therapy."

"Well, that's something. I guess I have no choice but to agree. I'm worried about him, though."

"Of course," she said softly.

Matthew ran his hand through his hair.

"Well, I'm glad he stepped up. This is good, right?"

"Yes. This is good news for everyone. I've been driving myself crazy working on this for a week and not doing anything else. I'm used to being in and out of the operating room, and I'm eager to get started on the surgeries."

Matthew cocked an eyebrow. "Well, I do have something else you can do. Something I was going to do myself, but since you've managed to finish with this, I think I can hand it over to you if you're interested."

"I'm intrigued."

Matthew handed her the file. "There's a living donor surgery this afternoon. It's a liver donation."

"Yes, that's great. I can help."

Matthew nodded. "I thought you might like that. It's a foster child and parent. The foster parent is planning to adopt the child after this procedure, but the little girl needs a liver donation due to extrahepatic cholestasis. She had a tumor, which damaged the biliary duct."

Victoria had tuned him out, because as soon as he'd said, "foster child and parent," she'd been triggered, and her hands began to shake as she went through the file. Every foster parent she had had was awful to her.

And she just couldn't imagine someone doing this for an orphan.

Just because you had an awful experience doesn't mean it's awful for everyone. Remember that.

She had to repeat that mantra in her head one more time.

Tears stung her eyes.

She was glad there was some positivity in this world.

"Are you okay?" Matthew asked.

"Why wouldn't I be?" she asked quietly.

"You seemed to freeze up, like you did in Mrs. Van Luven's surgery. You're trembling."

"Am I?" She glanced at her hands.

Matthew reached out and took her hands in hers. His hands were warm and strong. It calmed her.

She wanted him to hold her.

What're you doing?

She pulled her hands from his.

Victoria cleared her throat. "I'm fine. I would love to help with this, and I'll get right onto prepping them."

Matthew nodded. "Okay. I'll see you in a

bit. The surgery is set for five. Only this time, I lead."

Victoria nodded. "You're going to break the news to your brother about his donation?"

Matthew groaned. "I suppose so. Thank you for doing this."

She nodded again and left the office. Her heart was pounding, and she clutched the file for support.

You can do this.

All she had to do was bury all those emotions away. They wouldn't serve her in this situation. There were decent people in the foster system, and she often wondered what her life would've been like had she encountered some of them.

If she had had someone who cared about her.

She was envious of the start in life this little girl had, the support she was getting, but it was fleeting. Victoria had worked hard to get here, and she was going to do her job.

Like she always did.

CHAPTER SEVEN

MATTHEW WAS SO angry with Marcus as he stared at the report Victoria had brought to him. Volunteering for and becoming a living donor and complicating his domino surgery by inserting himself into the mix was ticking him off. And organ donation was a major surgery.

It was bad enough his brother had been harassing him about the surgery and when it would be organized, but now this? Now Marcus was becoming one of the donors? He could die. And the thought of losing someone else he loved was too much.

Matthew leaned back in his chair and scrubbed his hand over his face.

When had his life become so complicated?

It had been complicated when Kirsten got sick and had her short battle with cancer.

For a year he'd wandered around numb.

Lost.

He just existed. Work was his only escape. It was normal and steady.

But it wasn't normalcy. It was routine.

Either way, it was easy to do. It was easy to follow.

About a year ago, he'd tried to date again, but it was all wrong. He didn't go through with it, and he'd just accepted that he was going to be alone.

Which was fine.

He was used to it. He didn't want to experience that heartbreak again.

Since he'd taken his promotion to chief, his life had become increasingly more stressful. He didn't think it was the promotion or the domino that was making him anxious, so much as the appearance of Victoria back in his life. Something he hadn't been expecting. It was bad enough that he had been avoiding Victoria all week because he was angry at himself for allowing himself to be weak or having a moment of weakness when he took her in his arms and kissed her.

That moment—the one he'd thought about constantly for the last week, especially as he dodged her in the halls of Ziese Memorial Hospital—when he'd held her again had burned his soul. He'd dreamed of holding her since they'd parted ways, and in that moment that they were dancing and smiling on that rooftop patio, it was like no time had passed.

It had felt right.

And he didn't want it to feel that right.

Now Marcus had to go and interfere and play the hero in the surgery that Victoria was organizing.

Marcus is being unselfish and you're being a jerk!

He had to admit he was scared about his brother going through this life-changing surgery. In fact, truth be told, he kind of respected Marcus for offering up his kidney so that this surgery could happen, and Matthew felt like a fool for not realizing why.

Since he became chief, he hadn't had much time and so hadn't really looked closely at the domino patient profiles. He hadn't noticed that Jonas Fredrick was one of the recipients, and he was angry at himself for not catching that detail earlier.

Chase Fredrick was more Marcus's friend, but the Fredricks were friends of the Olesen family, and he'd known Jonas for a long time.

When Matthew had taken over as chief, he'd had a lot of fires to put out. Now, realizing it was Jonas, it made perfect sense why Marcus had been harping on at him and why his brother was stepping up to the plate to be a living donor.

He was going to have to apologize to Chase for not reaching out sooner.

Everything was just a mess, and this wasn't like him.

He usually had better control, and he hated that he was losing it.

There was another knock at the door, and he groaned inwardly.

Now what?

"Come."

Marcus poked his head in. "Vic's told you, then?"

"Vic?" Matthew asked. He didn't like the way Marcus called her Vic—Marcus's familiarity made his possessiveness prick.

"Victoria," Marcus responded, clearly noticing it irked him to hear Victoria called by the short form of her name.

"She doesn't like nicknames," he groused.

Which was true.

He'd tried it once—called her Vicky and received a bit of a tongue lashing from her in front of all the other residents.

"How do you know? Or did she tell you that over dinner?"

His stomach dropped to the soles of his feet. "What're you talking about?"

"She told me you had dinner last week and saw *Tryphine* in the Cay. So, naturally, I assumed she'd told you then."

"Yes," he said tightly, but then he sighed. "I've known Victoria for some time. We were residents together in New York."

Marcus quirked an eyebrow and came into his office and sat down. "You've slept with her, haven't you?"

Matthew clenched his jaw and his fists, which were resting on his lap under the desk. "I don't have time to talk to you about this, Marcus. I have a hospital to run."

Marcus smirked. "You so did."

"Grow up. That's not your business!"

Marcus smiled smugly. "Yep. You definitely have."

"What does it matter?" Matthew asked tersely.

"Well, you actually are a bit of a hot-blooded male after all. I thought you'd never move on from Kirsten."

Just the mention of his late wife's name

made his blood run cold. “And why should I move on from Kirsten?”

“Matthew, you deserve to be happy.”

Matthew stood up. He was done with the direction this conversation was taking. He didn’t want to be happy. He was perfectly fine.

No. You’re not.

“I have to prep for surgery. We’re done with this discussion.”

Marcus stood in front of him, blocking his exit. “Fine. You don’t want to talk about your feelings. What else is new? But you haven’t even told me if you’ve cleared me for surgery. It’s for Chase’s boy. Victoria had no problem with it. Do you?”

Matthew wanted to tell Marcus that he was worried for him. That he was scared, even, but he couldn’t, and he hated himself for it. For so long he’d looked out for Marcus. Taken care of him when his parents were off traveling or working.

And he was worried about this.

“Have you talked to Mom and Dad?”

“Yep, and they support me completely,” Marcus said.

“So they’re coming back home?” Matthew asked.

"No, I told them not to worry about it. I trust Victoria to do a great job, so there's no reason for them to worry or disrupt their cruise."

Matthew frowned. "They should be here."

"I'm fine. I don't need them here," Marcus said. "I can handle it. I know what I'm doing. They are worried, but it's okay. I reassured them."

Matthew cocked his eyebrow. "You reassured them? You know this surgery will change your life."

"I know. I understand what's involved," Marcus replied firmly. "Stop trying to parent me."

Matthew's heart softened a bit, but he didn't let his brother see that. "I'm not your keeper. You can do whatever you want with your kidneys. I'm clearing you for surgery."

"Thank you."

Matthew nodded as Marcus stepped away and left his office. He was angry that Marcus had brought up Victoria and Kirsten. That was none of his business. It shouldn't matter to his brother what his love life entailed.

Marcus had gone on about Matthew moving on before, and he knew Kirsten wouldn't want him to be alone. But the mention of Victoria…

The familiarity Marcus had with her and calling her Vic, making light of the love they'd shared when he didn't know the history…that rubbed Matthew the wrong way.

He shared that with no one.

That was his and his alone.

Matthew made his way down to the pre-operative floor. Victoria was already there, speaking with the liver donor and recipient. He could see her through the glass windows. Although the recipient looked a bit bored, he didn't blame her—she was only a child and probably didn't understand many of the technical words Victoria was saying.

Matthew watched her, and his heart melted. Why hadn't he stayed away from her like he said he would? He shouldn't have kissed her, but he couldn't help himself. That night had been magical. She had felt so good in his arms, and her lips had tasted as sweet as he remembered.

He couldn't distance himself from her professionally and didn't really want to. She was an excellent surgeon. He liked working with her. He'd missed working with her.

Their dinner last week had been a mistake, but that was a momentary lapse, and he wasn't going to make that mistake again.

Yeah. Right.

She got under his skin. He'd thought he was over Victoria, but he wasn't sure that he ever had gotten over her. Victoria left the room then, and he approached her. She immediately took a step back from him and made a face.

"What?" he asked.

"You have a face like thunder."

"Does thunder have a face?" he asked.

She tilted her head to the side. "Honestly, I don't know. I heard my… I heard that expression a lot when I was a kid but never really understood it."

She had clearly caught herself, and he wondered what she was going to say.

"I just had a discussion with Marcus, that's all. I'm fine with him being a living donor, but he likes to push my buttons, so I suppose that's why my face looks a bit annoyed."

"Well, the patients understand the procedure. They're ready. The residents should be back with the latest labs, but from reading their charts, I think they're both fit for surgery."

"Have you worked on a lot of pediatric patients before?" he asked.

"Not often, as we had a pediatric transplant surgeon in Manhattan, but I'm not unfamiliar with them," she said.

"Good. I'll work on prepping the recipient while you harvest the piece of liver from the donor."

Victoria nodded. "I'm fine with that."

"And when it's all done, it sounds like the little girl will have a loving home to be welcomed into."

"Yes." There was something off about her voice. As if something was bothering her. He noticed it when he gave her the file.

"Are you okay?"

"I'm fine. No face like thunder for me." She smiled, but the smile didn't reach her eyes. He could tell it was forced and he wasn't sure that he completely believed her, but it was none of his business.

As long as she did her job, it didn't matter. And he knew she was going to do excellent work. She was one of the best.

Now they were just standing there. Awkwardly.

"Look, we're okay, right?" Victoria asked frantically.

"How do you mean?"

She worried her bottom lip. “About last week...”

“We’re okay.”

“Good.”

“It won’t happen again.”

“You promise?” she asked.

“Yes.” Although part of him didn’t want to promise that. A part of him wanted more, but this wasn’t the place to talk about it.

He glanced over his shoulder and motioned for her to follow him into a small room so that no one could overhear them. It was bad enough that Marcus knew they’d had dinner together; he didn’t need the rest of the staff knowing his business. Once they were in the room, he shut the door.

“You don’t seem okay,” she said. “I’m sensing something is off.”

“I’m fine. I thought we worked this out? We both agreed that what happened was a mistake.”

“Yes, but I don’t want us to be estranged, either. I like working with you.”

“We’re not. We can be professionals.”

“You avoided me this week,” she stated.

Which was true. He had. “And you weren’t avoiding me?”

“Maybe.”

"So why worry?" he asked.

"When I was in Manhattan after the incident, I was ostracized, and it sucked. I don't want that to happen here."

He crossed his arms. "I thought you didn't care about what other surgeons thought?"

"I don't usually, but it doesn't feel so good when you're being purposefully avoided by others."

"I'm sorry."

"Good," she said. "And I'm sorry, too. I'm here to do my job, and I want to be able to do it well. I take pride in my work. It's the most important thing to me."

It was like a slap across the face from his past. Matthew was keenly aware how she felt about her job. He knew that she put her career first, because the last time she did that, his heart had suffered.

It had shattered.

And he was sure that it had never fully healed right.

Kirsten had helped, but he wasn't sure that he ever gave himself fully to her, as there was always a piece of himself that he had been holding back because he was so afraid of getting hurt. Well, he wasn't going to put himself in that kind of situation again.

"I know how much your job means to you," he said icily. "And I take my job as chief of surgery quite seriously, too."

"I know."

"Then we agree. Colleagues and friends. Nothing more."

She nodded. "Right."

He could see the pulse in her slender neck and noted that it was beating quite quickly. And suddenly he recalled that many of their most heated, passionate moments had started with a fight.

He might be hardening his heart, but there was nothing wrong with meaningless, detached sex, was there?

What is coming over you?

Matthew opened the door, desperate for an escape. "I'll see you in the scrub room?"

Victoria nodded quickly. "Yes. I look forward to working with you today, Dr. Olesen."

"Same, Dr. Jensen."

He left the room quickly. His body was reacting to her presence, and he had to make a mental note to not allow himself to be alone in a room with her again.

He refocused on the task at hand. It had been more than a week since he had done a surgery, which was unusual for him. He'd been so busy since he took over as chief, with paperwork to do, people to meet, balances and budgets to oversee, and he hadn't had a chance to step into the operating room.

Today's procedure was the kind of surgery he most liked to do. A live liver transplant was a win-win in his books. The donor's liver would grow back in time, and the recipient had a second chance at a healthy, happy life.

And since it was a young girl—a child—it was even better.

This was the best part of his job—saving a life.

Victoria was at the operating table, along with the rest of his staff.

An energy of hope passed through the room, and he took a deep, calming breath. This was what he liked to do just before he took hold of the scalpel.

Victoria watched him, her dark brown eyes keen and bright. He liked being here with her in an operating room. The first surgery they'd ever performed together hadn't been nearly as calm. He'd been in competition mode with a feisty, fiercely independent, beautiful surgical resident named Victoria back then.

As they'd worked side by side, he'd been aware of her talent and worried about his own position in the program. Just as he was worried about his attraction to her. How much he wanted her.

Now there was no fight for a spot. He was in charge. Although that undercurrent of sexual attraction was still there. He was hoping it wasn't, but it was. What was it about her that ensnared him so?

"You ready, Dr. Olesen?" she asked, standing next to him.

"I am, Dr. Jensen."

The scrub nurse handed him the scalpel, and he went to work to harvest a healthy piece of liver. Victoria stepped up as an assist, and for the first time in a long time, he didn't have to explain anything to the other surgeon.

She anticipated his moves, and they worked together seamlessly.

She was flawless.

It had been a long time since he'd worked with a surgeon of Victoria's caliber. He had missed this.

It was comfortable.

It was familiar.

It was like coming home.

"This is a healthy liver," Victoria murmured as she worked.

"It is."

"The girl is lucky to have such amazing foster parents." There was a bit of censure in her voice, and her hands trembled ever so slightly.

"Are you okay, Dr. Jensen?" he asked, worried she'd freeze up again.

He knew how much her experience in New York City must have traumatized her. He could tell from Mrs. Van Luven's surgery it was still affecting her.

And he understood trauma. It had been hard for him to walk in the oncology ward for a couple years with the memory of Kirsten haunting those halls.

"I'm fine," she said quickly. "I'm okay to do this."

"Well, it's a pleasure to work with you again."

She cocked an eyebrow. "And it was a pleasure to work together when we were residents and fighting for position in that program."

"Of course, the others weren't a threat. You were because of your talent. I appreciate talent."

"Why, thank you, Dr. Olesen."

"You sound surprised."

"You've never said that to me before. Ever."

He smiled. "Well, it's deserved. And you're welcome."

She snorted in response, and he chuckled.

What're you doing? a little voice in Matthew's head asked. He kept telling himself he had to keep his distance from her. The problem was, he couldn't.

He missed her camaraderie.

Her friendship.

Her body.

All this time and the rift between them hadn't changed a thing.

He missed her.

Victoria was exhausted. Her body ached, and she felt like her feet were cement blocks. She sat down on the floor of the surgeons' changing room and rested her head against her knees. The surgery had gone well, but she was emotionally wrung out.

When had her life become so complicated?

She was so glad the little girl had pulled through. That little girl had a new liver, and she would have a mom and dad who cared for her.

She had a chance.

Something Victoria had never had.

She was envious of that little girl's good fortune.

She'd wake up from her surgery and she'd have a family.

Victoria had never had a family, but it was something she always secretly wanted.

Whereas Matthew had a brother and parents, yet he seemed to have no desire to be around them.

She didn't get it.

It was obvious he was cared for and loved. And she wondered what that was like.

You could've known if you hadn't pushed Matthew away.

Matthew walked into the changing room and paused.

"You okay?" he asked.

No.

Except she didn't say that. "Just tired. It was a long surgery."

"Yeah, but it went well."

She nodded. "I was a foster child."

He seemed shocked. "You were?"

And she couldn't quite believe the words were coming out. "You asked me before why I seemed off, and it's because I grew up in the system."

Matthew's expression softened, and he

came to sit beside her on the floor. "What happened to your parents?"

"My mother died when I was ten. I have very small, fragmented memories of her. You know those kinds of memories that are orange-hued and faded?"

He smiled. "Yeah. What about your father?"

"I never knew him, so I was put in the foster system when my mother died."

"I'm sorry. That's horrible."

She shrugged. Numb. She never cried and she wasn't going to start now, but she felt relief sharing this with him. Like it was a huge weight off her chest.

"Not all foster parents are bad. Most aren't," he said softly.

"I know. I've met wonderful people since then, but that wasn't my experience growing up." She sighed. "I'm exhausted."

And she was. There had been a lot going on since she'd come here to St. Thomas, and she felt like she was crashing from it all.

Like she was free falling.

"You need to go home and get some rest."

"Right." She stood, and Matthew got up, too. "I better call a cab. I usually just walk, but it's midnight."

"I'll drive you."

"I thought we weren't going to get involved with each other."

"We're not. A friend can drive a friend home."

She should say no and just take a cab, but she wanted to be friends with Matthew. She'd missed her friend.

"Okay. I'll grab my stuff and meet you in the lobby."

"Sounds good," he said as he left the room.

Victoria quickly got out of her surgical scrubs and back into her street clothes. She grabbed her stuff from the boardroom where she worked and made her way to the lobby, where Matthew was waiting for her. They walked out to his car, and she climbed in, her body relaxing against the supple leather of the interior.

"Where do you live again?" he asked. "I somewhat remember, but I'm not exactly sure."

"In the condos at the end of A Street."

"Right. That sounds familiar. I know those places."

It wasn't a long drive, but she was appreciative of his offer when he pulled up in front of the building where she was staying.

"Thanks for the lift."

"It's no problem." He smiled. "What're your plans for tomorrow? I know it's your day off."

"I don't know. I haven't had a day off yet. I don't usually take time off."

"I remember. I think you need to see St. Thomas."

"What?"

"You took me on that tour of New York City when I first arrived. This is payback! If you recall, I didn't really want to go on that tour."

Victoria groaned and then smiled as she thought of that tour of Manhattan she'd taken him on and how he grumbled through it all, though she'd known he was just teasing her. She knew they'd both had had a lot of fun. It had been one of those halcyon memories she cherished. They had seen the Statue of Liberty and Rockefeller Center and gone to the Top of the Rock. They had been to Central Park and Times Square. They had done all the real touristy stuff.

She usually didn't do things like that, and that day with Matthew had been one of the best, goofiest days of her life.

She hadn't thought about it in so long.

You shouldn't go.

But the part of her that wanted to go was stronger.

She was lonely and stressed out, and she just wanted some fun so that she could try to forget everything that had happened to her in Manhattan.

“Fine,” she said grudgingly, but with a smile so he didn’t think she was a total grump. “If it’s payback, then I guess I have no choice but to accompany you.”

Matthew nodded. “Right. I’ll pick you up at nine?”

“Sure. That sounds good.” She climbed out of the car and shut the door.

Matthew waved and drove off.

Her stomach started to do that flip-flop it always did whenever she was around him.

She should stay home.

She should’ve turned him down, but for the first time, she wondered if maybe she didn’t have to be alone.

And it scared her.

CHAPTER EIGHT

VICTORIA HADN'T SLEPT a wink.

Between telling Matthew about her childhood, which no one knew about, their kiss and this domino surgery, her mind was racing a hundred miles a minute.

She was tossing and turning all night as she imagined about what today would bring. There were times she thought this was a bad idea and then other times she was excited about spending a day with Matthew.

Even though she didn't deserve to feel excited about being with him again. Not when she had hurt him all those years ago.

Spending her day off with him was not keeping her distance from him. Only she couldn't help herself. She was lonely. She usually always had her work to distract her, but here, other than planning the domino, she had nothing else, and so it was just her and her loneliness.

What else have you got to do?

Victoria eventually gave up with her waffling back and forth, put on a light, airy sundress and made her way outside when it was time for him to pick her up. She didn't know what today was going to bring, but she was going to go with the flow, which wasn't her usual tactic. She was hoping she'd be able to relax and calm her mind. The sun was bright and warm, but there was a gentle breeze blowing, and it helped break the heat.

It was a perfect day in paradise. A day in paradise with Matthew. Her stomach did a flip.

It was just a day out with a friend.

She could spend a day with an old friend.

Nothing had to happen.

Nothing would happen!

Matthew pulled up in his Audi, and as she climbed into the passenger seat, it felt like butterflies had taken over her entire abdomen. She was so nervous being around him, which was a first, and she knew it was because of what she'd shared with him. He knew about her past.

He knew too much about her. It made her

wary, even if there was a part of her that liked him knowing that about her. It was like a huge weight off her shoulders.

"Good morning! You look nice," he complimented.

"Thanks." Her cheeks bloomed with heat. "You look great, too."

And he did. He was wearing khaki pants and a light blue cotton shirt. She loved that color of blue on him. It brought out the color of his eyes.

Eyes she had gotten lost in time and time again.

"How do you feel about boat rides?" he asked.

"Did you convince your brother to lend you the *Tryphine*?" she asked, confused.

Matthew snorted. "No. I was thinking more of a ferry ride."

She didn't like boats at the best of times. "I've ridden the ferries in New York. Are you taking me to St. John, since your brother is here?" she teased. She wouldn't mind doing some island hopping. Work in New York kept her busy, and she didn't take much time off. She wanted to travel around the islands a bit before she went back to her lonesome life in Manhattan.

"No, I thought you might like to go to St. Croix. See where I grew up."

Her stomach knotted and then dropped like a rock to the soles of her feet. "You're taking me to see your parents?"

"No." He laughed. "They're not home. They're on a round-the-world cruise, but I have been tasked with checking on their place from time to time, and I thought it was a good time to show you the island."

"How long is this ferry ride?"

"About ninety minutes or so."

"What?" she choked.

"You'll have plenty of time to visit St. Thomas, as it's pretty easy to see most of the island. St. John and Water Island aren't far from Charlotte Amalie, but to get the full Virgin Islands experience, you'll have to go to St. Croix."

"So we're island hopping today?" she asked cautiously.

He grinned, his eyes twinkling. "Yes. We are. And you can experience the luxury car my dad leaves parked at the Gallows Bay Dock."

"Oh, so it's not a car ferry?"

"No. Just a passenger ferry," Matthew

said as he pulled up to the ferry terminal at French Town.

Victoria could see the little bistro where he'd taken her out to dinner, in particular that rooftop where he had pulled her into a dance that ended with a kiss. One that she still couldn't stop thinking about, even though she knew she had to.

They had already decided that the kiss was a mistake.

But there was a part of her that felt like it hadn't been.

It had felt *right*.

It had felt like something that had been missing. And this line of thinking wasn't going to help her keep her distance from him. It just made her want him more.

Matthew parked the car and then came around to open her door for her. She followed him as he walked up to the ticket booth and bought two round-trip tickets from Charlotte Amalie to Christiansted on St. Croix.

The ferry didn't look like the big ferries that she was used to seeing in New York City. This one reminded her of a tourist sightseeing boat, and she paused. It seemed a bit small for open water. Matthew turned around.

"Nervous?"

"I'm okay with larger vessels. Not sure how I'll feel about this." Her voice shook slightly.

Matthew smiled and held out his hand. "It'll be fine. I promise you."

Victoria slipped her hand in his as they boarded.

"Do you want to sit up on deck?" he asked.

"Yes. I think that might be better. That way if I feel ill, I can just run to the side of the boat."

He chuckled. "I swear, you'll be fine, and the sea air will do you good."

Victoria wasn't sure, but she didn't let go of his hand as she followed him to the upper deck, where there were bench seats. Her hand in his felt right. His hand was strong and reassuring, and she didn't want to let it go.

And as they sat there, she still held on to him, like it was the most natural thing in the world. Like he was her security. Just like when she had frozen in the operating room and he'd talked her through and when he'd held her hand before she told him about her past. It calmed her nerves.

She was safe with him.

She'd only ever felt that safety with her mother.

So long ago.

They found a bench to themselves near the back and settled in as the ferry continued to load. Matthew didn't try to pull away, either. Neither of them said anything as they sat there together. The only sound was the water lapping against the hull and buzzing talk of boarding passengers.

It wasn't long before the moorings were pulled up and the green-and-white vessel made its way out into the Cay and toward St. Croix.

The turquoise waters gave way to the darker blue of the deep Virgin Islands trough of the Caribbean Sea. Victoria didn't say much, because she wasn't sure if she could speak over the sound of the wind and the water.

Or if her churning stomach would let her.

Matthew didn't seem to mind as he stared out over the water, his arm draped along the back of the bench. Even though his arm wasn't around her, she found it reassuring that he was there, and she slid a bit closer, enjoying the sight of St. Thomas slipping away and keeping her eyes fixed on the horizon line, waiting for that first glimpse of St. Croix.

The sun felt good.

It had been a long time since she'd sat out in the sun and just drunk in the vitamin D.

Usually, she was too busy at the hospital, but there were rare times when a nice spring day would hit the city and she would sneak off to Central Park to sit out and listen to the city and enjoy the outside.

It was a peaceful voyage, and the ninety minutes it took seemed to slip by. Soon she could see the sliver of the island of St. Croix looming in the distance—the lush greenery and vibrantly colored roofs as they approached Gallows Bay.

"See," Matthew said. "That wasn't so bad, was it?"

"No. You're right. When is the next ferry back?"

"Already trying to escape me?" he teased.

"No. I just want to make sure we don't miss it. We have a lot of work tomorrow."

He cocked his eyebrow. "We? The domino surgery is yours."

"Fine, me, then. Are you happy?"

"I am." He smiled smugly, and she laughed.

She didn't mind that the domino was hers to coordinate. It had been a long time since she had organized one. Since becoming a full-fledged attending, she'd had her own residents to do much of the grunt work.

Matthew glanced at his watch as he stood. "Four. It's ten now, so we have a couple hours to kill. Better make the most of it."

Victoria nodded, and they disembarked.

She followed him as they headed to a parking garage that wasn't far from the Gallows Bay terminal, and he pulled out a fob to a Lamborghini that was hiding in the shadows, but it wasn't like a usual one. It was an open-topped speed car. It looked kind of monstrous.

It was like nothing she'd ever seen before.

"Your father drives that?" Victoria asked, shocked.

Matthew nodded. "I know. Wait until you see the modest homestead."

"Is it far from here?" She was worried about the trip back to St. Thomas.

"About twenty minutes."

She nodded and climbed into the car. What else was she going to do—hang around the docks worrying about getting back to Charlotte Amalie and Ziese Memorial Hospital?

She had to trust Matthew.

Matthew started the engine and the car

revved to life, making her body quiver with a bit of excitement as he grinned at her.

"You ready?" he asked.

"I think so."

He slipped on his shades and drove out of the parking garage and out onto the streets of Christiansted. He made his way slowly through traffic and then headed east, where he allowed the speed to creep up.

She started to laugh as the wind whipped at her face as he sped along winding roads, the urban center dropping away to be replaced by country homes and farms. The sea disappeared as they tracked south through lush greenery and fields, and they passed through towns like Sally's Fancy and Madame Carty before the road turned and they were climbing up a hill, the water below them. It gave her a thrill, feeling as though they were racing along the edge.

Every so often she'd catch a glimpse of a serene-looking white beach, she wished she could walk through the soft sand and swim in the turquoise waters.

Matthew pulled off the main road and took another long, windy road up a mountain until the trees gave way and she spied what looked almost like a Spanish castle sitting on top of the hill. Her mouth dropped open at the sight of the white-domed structure.

"You lived in a castle as a child?"

Matthew chuckled. "Yes. I told you, my father likes things big."

"I thought you were teasing," she mumbled. "I don't know why I thought you were teasing."

He laughed as he slowed to a stop at the gate and punched in the security code. The gate slowly opened, and he crept along the long drive until they were in front of the house.

He parked the car. "Welcome to the Olesen homestead."

Victoria got out of the car and stared. The view from where the home was seated was spectacular—there was a vista every direction you looked, and she felt like it would be the perfect place to watch for pirates.

"Wow" was all she could say.

"Yeah, again, my father is not a subtle man. He grew up in Denmark, in a very small apartment in Copenhagen. He had to be crammed in there with his siblings, so this is his compensation for that. At least, that's what he's always told us."

She chuckled. “I can see that.”

“Come. I’ll show you around.” He held out his hand again, and she took it naturally, without thinking. It felt right to hold his hand.

They walked into the house, and there were marble and gilded ceilings, with a large winding staircase that led up to the dome.

It was open, and her voice echoed as she stared up at it.

“Come on, I’ll show you the patio, because it’s my favorite place.”

“The patio is your favorite place?” she teased. “All of this and the patio is what you like?”

“I’m a simple man. My father, not so much.” He grinned. “Come on.”

She followed him out under the staircase to a pair of French doors. He let go of her hand to open them, and she gasped at the white stone and the complete, unobstructed view of the Caribbean Sea.

An infinity pool clung to the edge and seemed to mix in with sea and sky. The edge of the pool had a translucent side, so it felt like you were swimming over a cliff. It was stunning. At the far end of the pool was a hot tub and a waterfall.

It was like something from a resort.

The entrance to the large pool sloped like you were walking into the ocean, and there was even sand.

"Would you like a swim?" he asked. "It is quite something swimming on the edge of a cliff under a castle."

"Okay, this definitely tops the Statue of Liberty," she murmured in awe.

He grinned. "No, you can't compare the two. That was impressive, too. The tall buildings of New York making you feel so small. It was the edge of America, or that's how I felt standing there."

"Sure, but this is like something out of that show that showed how the überrich always lived. One of my foster mothers was obsessed with how the far wealthier lived."

"Our house was on that show. Of course, it wasn't as impressive as it is now."

She looked at him in disbelief. "You're not serious?"

He grinned, his blue eyes twinkling. "No. I'm not serious. My father likes his showpieces, but he's also very private, too. He's a bit of a paradox."

Victoria laughed. “I find that hard to believe.”

“Do you want to have a swim or not?” he asked, crossing his arms.

“I would, but I don’t have a bathing suit.”

“My mother has tons of them. She even has guest ones in the pool house. Grab a suit and change in there, and I’ll grab us some drinks and snacks.”

“Fine,” she said. She wouldn’t mind having a swim in that luxurious pool. When would she have the chance to experience a pool like this again? Probably never. Matthew opened the door to the pool house, which was a white stucco building that looked more like a small cottage than a pool house. She shut the door behind her and saw it was indeed set out like a cottage with a cozy living room and gleaming teak floors.

There was a modern kitchenette and a small, luxurious bathroom. She eventually found the master bedroom, which had one of those beds that she always pictured in the Caribbean, with the beautiful netting, and when she opened the French doors there was a tiny little balcony that overlooked the sea.

She took a deep breath, breathing in the fresh sea air.

She could definitely get used to this.

Not the massive home, but a small house like this next to the sea. The little dream caught her off guard, because she'd never really thought about something like that.

She never really dared to dream of something other than her career and New York.

There were times in her life when she'd allowed herself to dream, and those dreams were always crushed.

She'd always dreamed of having a loving home.

Security.

Safety.

But as each year went by and no one adopted her, Victoria eventually stopped dreaming.

With a sigh she headed back into the room, shutting the doors and finding the wardrobe full of bathing suits.

Nothing in black, which was her usual color.

It was all white.

And all two-pieces.

Victoria swallowed the lump in her throat.

He's seen you naked before.

She swallowed her fear and picked up a

two-piece and changed. All they were doing was going for a swim.

Two friends swimming.

That was all.

Matthew changed into a pair of swimming trunks and set out the lemonade and the fruit salad he'd found in the kitchen. He'd called the house staff yesterday and told them he was coming with a friend when he got this brilliant idea to bring Victoria out here on his biweekly check on his parents' estate.

His parents had staff, but they still insisted Matthew or Marcus come every once in a while.

Although Marcus never did.

Matthew was the responsible one. His parents always expected it, so he couldn't let them down. Although it would be nice if Marcus stepped up occasionally.

Don't think about Marcus now.

Marcus would bug him about how bringing a woman out here was a recipe for seduction. Well, that might be his twin brother's usual operation, but it wasn't his. He didn't bring women here.

And when he was with Kirsten, they had been too busy working to come here as often as they'd liked. Then she had been too sick to travel.

He could see why Marcus brought women here.

And he understood why his dad had built something like this—it was opulent, and his parents both liked showing off.

He didn't particularly like showing off. He preferred his modest-size home just outside Charlotte Amalie with a private beach.

That's not really much different. You have your own beach.

He set down the tray, and the pool house door opened.

"Would you like a..." His voice trailed off as Victoria came out in a white bikini. Suddenly he couldn't breathe. It was like he'd been punched and all the air had been forced out of his body.

"Would I like a what?" she asked, tying back her long, silky brown hair.

Say something.

Except all he could hear was the pounding of his pulse between his ears.

"Iced tea?" he asked, finally finding his voice.

"Yes. Thank you." She made her way over to the table, and he poured her a glass. He was hoping his hand wasn't shaking and tried not to look at her. Suddenly, he felt like a dorky young man again. All awkward and uncomfortable around his crush.

She took a seat, and he sat on the other side of the table, staring out over the blue water.

"This is beautiful, but you know, when you told me that we were going to do touristy stuff I thought you were going schlep me around a bunch of old forts and tourist traps."

He cocked an eyebrow. "Is that what you want to do?"

She laughed softly. "No. This is better. I didn't realize how stressed I actually was until now."

"Agreed. It's been some time since I came out here and enjoyed the sun."

"You okay?" she asked.

"I was just thinking about my late wife. She loved it here."

"I can see why," Victoria said. "Do you mind me asking how she died?"

"No." He wasn't sure he wanted to talk about it, but also there was a part of him that did because he was tired of holding it all in. There was no point in hiding it—Victoria knew he was a widower. "It was cervical and ovarian cancer. By the time they discovered it, it was too late. She was gone six months later. She was only thirty-two."

"I'm sorry. She was so young."

He nodded. "She was."

"We were only married for a couple of years, but after she died, I threw myself into my work. I took every surgery I could, filled my roster up, and I guess that's why the board of directors offered me the position to become chief of surgery."

"I can see that. That's kind of how I rose to the top. Work and only work. It's easier to work than deal with…other things."

"I remember," he said dryly. "You were very focused on work."

"Well, work provided security. Work meant that I had a roof on my head and I wouldn't starve."

A pang of guilt washed over him. It all made perfect sense.

She had no one, and he'd grown up like this.

His parents had been absent a lot, but his parents loved him and made sure that he was provided for. He didn't have debt when he came out of school. There was never a night that he had to go hungry or worry about a roof over his head. Still, his parents left him and Marcus a lot. Which was why Matthew often felt more like a parent than a brother. He hadn't really had a childhood, either. Suddenly, he understood Victoria just a little bit better.

He felt closer to her.

"Okay, enough of this," he stated, setting his glass down. "I'm going swimming."

He made his way over to the pool and wandered in. The water was cool and refreshing. It had been a long time since he'd gone swimming, and he paddled to the edge of the infinity pool, glancing down at the ocean below him.

He turned around, expecting Victoria to follow him. "Are you coming?"

"Yeah, I like wading, but I don't know how to swim."

"What?"

"I grew up in the system. Swimming lessons weren't part of my upbringing." She got up and gingerly made her way into the water. He swam over to her.

"Do you want me to show you?" Matthew asked.

"I don't know," she said nervously.

"Come on." He held out his hand. She slipped her hand in his, and he gently guided her into the water until she was up to her waist. She was trembling. "It's okay."

"Are you sure?" she asked.

"Positive. This is also a saltwater pool—it's more buoyant." He pulled her into the deeper water, closer to the edge.

Victoria threw her arms around his neck.

His pulse began to race having her so close, and he held her as she freaked out slightly.

"This is crazy," she said, her voice on edge.

"It's not. Everyone swims."

"Not me."

"It'll be fine, look." And he swam over to the edge and disengaged her limbs from around him and had her hold on to the side of the pool. Her eyes were closed. "Kick your legs and you'll stay up."

She nodded and opened one eye. "Oh, wow."

"See. It's worth it."

She nodded, gripping the edge. "Okay, maybe I can get used to this swimming thing."

He chuckled and they floated there, on the edge of the pool, watching the ocean. It was so peaceful. Why was it so right with Victoria? Why did he keep getting sucked into something with her? Why couldn't he stay away from her?

It didn't have to be anything. It could just be this. It could just be this moment as friends.

He could be her friend, but he wanted to be more with her. A year after Kirsten died, his brother and his parents had tried to get him to move on, but he had never been interested in anyone else.

He'd tried to go on a date, but it was just never right, and that was the end of it.

He really didn't have any desire to continue anything.

No one ever really sparked any interest in him.

The only two women in his life who had done that were Kirsten and Victoria. And for so long he'd thought both women were gone, out of his life for good.

"Why would your parents want to leave this to see the world?" Victoria teased. "This is paradise."

Matthew laughed. "I know. They don't stay put too much. Even when I was a kid."

"Who looked after you and Marcus?" she asked.

"Nannies," Matthew responded. "Or boarding school, or me, but when they were here, it was home."

She smiled, but he could see the sadness in her eyes. He could see the pain and longing. It was a different side to her, and it made him want to reach out and take her in his arms.

To protect her.

He didn't want her to feel that pain of loneliness anymore.

"Thanks for bringing me here. I actually think this really isn't fair."

He cocked an eyebrow. "How do you mean?"

"Well, you said the tour would be payback, and you were implying that my tour was terrible. This is lovely."

He grinned. "I'm glad you're enjoying some downtime. I can still take you to the fort if you'd like?"

"Pass." She laughed. "I wouldn't mind some lunch somewhere, though. The fruit salad was nice, but I'm still hungry."

"Want to take another ride?" he asked.

"I hope you mean in the car."

A zing of anticipation ran through him, and he moved closer to her. "Of course."

"Well, help me get out of this pool."

Matthew took her in his arms, his body reacting to holding her body so close to his as he helped her swim until her feet could touch the bottom of the pool again. He didn't want to let go of her, but it was for the best.

He needed to put some distance between them.

Although, as she waded out of the pool, he couldn't help but notice her curves, and he recalled being able to touch every inch of her, making her quiver with pleasure.

That was a long time ago.

And he had to keep reminding himself of that, because he couldn't stand getting close to her and losing her again.

He couldn't take another loss, even though he was so tempted to have just one more night with her. To have her in his arms again.

The rest of the day passed in a blur.

After their swim in the pool, something had changed between them. Victoria wasn't sure what, but it was probably for the best. When they had been in the pool and his arms had been around her, she'd felt something.

Terror, but also something else.

Similar to that heat, that electric pull, she'd felt when they had been dancing on the rooftop and they'd kissed. It was probably best that they got out of the pool and left his parents' opulent castle on top of the hill.

He drove them down the mountain to a small bistro just outside Christiansted, and their entire conversation had been about work.

Which was so much safer.

Now they were back on the ferry, headed back to St. Thomas.

Except this time, Matthew wasn't sitting next to her. He was leaning on the railing and staring out over the water.

Her purse began to vibrate, and she pulled out her phone.

"Hello?" she answered, confused.

"Dr. Jensen? It's Dr. Gainsbourg from Ziese Memorial Hospital."

"Yes, Dr. Gainsbourg?" As soon as she said his name, Matthew glanced over his shoulder at her.

"It's about the domino."

Her stomach sank like a rock. She'd done this enough times to know that there were a few different things that could go wrong at this stage. Donors could pull out or a recipient could pass away. "We lost a donor, didn't we?"

Matthew spun around, his brow furrowed, his arms crossed.

"We've lost two. The domino surgery is

collapsing," Dr. Gainsbourg stated. "It's a mess right now."

"Thank you. We'll be back as soon as we can, and I'll deal with it." She ended the call and worried her bottom lip.

"It's the surgery, isn't it?" Matthew asked. She could hear the edge in his voice. "It's falling apart, right?"

"It is. Two donors have pulled out. We need to fix this."

CHAPTER NINE

VICTORIA POURED HERSELF another cup of coffee and stared at her whiteboard. Seven days—a whole week ago—her domino had fallen apart, and she still hadn't been able to set it right yet. As soon as the ferry docked at Charlotte Amalie, she'd headed straight for the hospital and tried to get more testing done, to find other matches out of the willing pool of incompatible donors.

She had found one replacement donor, but she was having a hard time finding a second. Mrs. Van Luven was rapidly deteriorating and the young boy Marcus was worried about, the reason he'd stepped up to become a living donor, was also in rough shape—Jonas had been transferred to Ziese Memorial Hospital from St. John because he needed to be monitored and his dialysis was no longer working.

It worried Victoria that two of the recipients were now hospitalized and both were receiving peritoneal dialysis over hemodialysis.

She just needed one more donor, just one more match to step up, and then she could get the domino up and running. She had her team of surgeons waiting. There were so many people in the wings ready for this to be a go.

Matthew wandered into the boardroom, and she noted that he had bags under his eyes as well. She knew that he had been just as stressed as she was since the domino surgery had fallen apart.

"Any luck?" he asked, a hopeful tone to his voice.

"No. I still need another donor, and I'm running out of time." She sighed. "I'm hoping someone steps up, but I get it. It's a surgery, and it's a big deal."

"Jonas is stable, and he's taking to the peritoneal dialysis well," Matthew stated, sitting down in a chair across from her.

"That's at least something. Mrs. Van Luven is somewhat stable, but she needs the surgery soon."

"I've contacted UNOS. I know it's a long shot, but if we can get a kidney from a deceased donor, then we can do a five-way live donor domino."

"It's worth a shot."

She didn't have high hopes. There were still people ahead on the list, but they had to try something.

Anything.

"How is Marcus doing? Did he pass his counseling?" Matthew asked.

"He did. He's been cleared."

Matthew frowned.

"I thought you'd be happy," Victoria said. "You wanted him to have a clear conscience before he made the decision to have the surgery, and he does."

"He's grown man, but…he's my twin brother." He gave her a half smile. "I can't help but worry."

"As you say, he's a grown man. You don't need to parent him."

"I don't parent him. He's just… He drives me crazy."

"Maybe you do have feelings for your brother?" she teased.

"You're exhausted and saying foolish things," he groused.

"How do you know that? I said I was stressed, not tired."

"You look tired," he murmured, purposely changing the subject.

"So do you."

"I have a hospital to run, and I want this surgery to be a success, too." He scrubbed a hand over his face. "Explain to me again why those two donors pulled out of it in the first place?"

"One was too scared, and the other is moving overseas. They got a big promotion and have to move soon."

Matthew raised his eyebrows. "We could write a doctor's note for the donor who has to move for a job, or maybe we can convince one of the donors to come back?" he asked. "One of the original ones who dropped out when we had our matches."

"That's against every procedure under UNOS and would jeopardize this surgery. We can't try to persuade a donor and you know it. Even if I want to so badly."

"I know. It's frustrating, but I understand."

Dr. Gainsbourg came into the room just then, his face grim. "Dr. Jensen?"

"It's Mrs. Van Luven. Her numbers are deteriorating, aren't they?" she asked, her heart sinking.

Dr. Gainsbourg nodded. "I managed to get her stable, but I thought you'd like to see the report."

Victoria nodded and took the report from the younger doctor.

The numbers confirmed her fears, and suddenly this felt like what had happened with the ambassador…

"I don't think I can operate on the ambassador. Not with numbers like this."

"The board of directors would like you to. The ambassador knows you are the best, and this would be an absolute coup for this hospital if you did. This would completely advance your career. Isn't that what you want?" Paul asked earnestly.

Victoria stared at the report.

"I'll try," she said, even though her every instinct was telling her this wasn't safe.

Victoria shook that memory from her mind. What she should've said was that she didn't feel comfortable and she should've walked away from that surgery.

Why didn't she listen to herself? Why was she so desperate to please Dr. Martin and the board of directors?

She hated herself for that, but she'd learned something, too. She was going to always go with her instincts. Numbers on lab reports didn't lie. Sure, miracles happened, but she was never, ever going to put a patient at risk ever again.

Medicine wasn't a business to her.

It was life.

And it was clear from the lab report that it wouldn't be much longer until she couldn't do a surgery on Mrs. Van Luven. Her body would be too weak and wouldn't be able to handle the transplant.

"Thanks, Dr. Gainsbourg. Keep me posted on her condition."

Dr. Gainsbourg nodded.

"What're we going to do?" Victoria asked.

Matthew shook his head. "I don't know. The only way this surgery works is if everyone is involved. If Mrs. Van Luven doesn't get a kidney, her donor won't give to the next person. You know how it goes."

"Except that Marcus is Mrs. Van Luven's donor. The question is, would your brother still donate the kidney even if this whole thing falls apart?"

"I don't know. And we can't ask that of him," Matthew responded quietly.

"I hope UNOS calls. I hope we can find an answer soon." She sighed and stared out the window. "What I wouldn't give to go for a swim in your parents' pool right about now and maybe have some rum punch, too."

He chuckled. "I have been thinking about that myself. Although drinking and swimming isn't that wise."

"I never did thank you for that day," she said softly. "We got back to Charlotte Amalie, and this whole surgery fell apart and I've been scrambling since."

"I know. So have I." He stood up and wandered over to stand beside her. "Has the situation in New York blown over yet?"

The question caught her off guard. It suddenly felt like he was trying to get rid of her.

Her spine stiffened, and she worried her bottom lip. "Not exactly. I got an email from the board of directors saying that the autopsy findings have been published and my name has officially been cleared."

Matthew's brow furrowed. "So you're leaving?"

"No. I'm going to finish the domino and see it through. I don't leave jobs unfinished, so I'll stay here until it's done."

Relief washed over his expression. "I'm glad to hear it, but won't New York want you back as soon as possible?"

"There's no rush. The press is still circling,

and the board did add that they were thrilled with the domino surgery I'm undertaking here in this little hospital. Though it's hardly little."

"St. Thomas is part of the United States. We even have some their big box stores here," he said jokingly.

"I know, but if it's not Manhattan, then it's 'little' to them." She smiled. "Eventually this surgery will be over and I'll be able to return to my practice."

A strange expression crossed his face. "You'll return to New York?"

"You just asked me about my job. Why wouldn't I go back?

"You could go somewhere else," he hinted.

"Where?" she asked, amused.

Matthew shrugged. "Anywhere."

He was right. What would happen if she didn't return to New York? She could go anywhere, except there was a niggling thought at the back of her mind.

Even though she knew the autopsy results had cleared her of all fault, the bad press wouldn't exactly gain her new patients for a while, and if she wasn't earning money, what board of directors would take her on?

Probably not many.

Matthew might.

She was lucky to be here, but this wasn't where she was supposed to be. She wouldn't risk her heart or his. It was better to be alone. Alone was safer than risking it on something foolish like love, so she'd return to New York. Ultimately, she knew she was too scared to leave the security of the city of her birth—the city she'd shared with her mom before she'd died.

She cleared her throat, trying to break the tension. "No, I'll go back to New York."

Matthew seemed disappointed with her answer, but he didn't say anything further. "Well, I need to check on my other patients. If I hear anything from UNOS, I'll let you know."

"Thanks."

Matthew nodded and left.

She sighed, frustrated. New York City was the only home she knew. Yet there was a part of her that didn't want to go back.

You could stay?

Only it was obvious from Matthew's suggestion that she could go anywhere. After this domino and her time in St. Thomas were over, she wouldn't be able to stay here. He hadn't exactly asked her to.

Do you blame him?

She'd hurt him so badly ten years ago.

The thing was, it had hurt her, too, when she pushed him away. It had been ten years, and she still wanted him.

It scared her how he made her feel safe again. It had been a long time since she'd felt that security. Not since she was a child and her mother had been alive. Not that she remembered much, but there were those small, happy memories. And then those memories of her time with Matthew. She had ruined their love.

It was her fault, and though she wanted that back, she was so afraid it could be taken away from her again.

That she'd lose him because she loved him too much.

Even though she had been completely stressed about this surgery falling apart, she couldn't stop thinking about their time on St. Croix. How safe he had made her feel on the ferry and when they were in the pool together. His touch grounded her, and when she was with him she felt like she could do anything.

She had been so self-conscious when she walked out of the pool house in that bikini, but then when she saw him, all of that melted away, and when he held her in the water in his strong arms, her body melted.

It had taken all her willpower not to kiss him.

And when she was relaxing at the edge of that pool, all she could think about was how wonderful it would be to take him into that lovely small room in the pool house and fall into that big, beautiful bed.

Heat bloomed in her cheeks.

She was obviously tired, because she usually had better control over her emotions than this. Except she was losing control. She loved being here in Charlotte Amalie and working with Matthew. She didn't feel so alone.

She had her best friend back.

She had her lover back.

Heat rushed through her as she thought of their first time together. She would give anything to experience that heady, pleasure-filled night again.

Even if it was a bad idea.

"Victoria?"

She turned as Matthew came back in the room. Her heart skipped a beat, her body trembling as she gazed at him.

What could it hurt to indulge in one night again?

When he had kissed her on that rooftop, she'd pushed him away, but she knew that he was feeling it, too. She knew that Matthew wanted her just as much as she wanted him.

They weren't strangers. They were both adults.

She closed the gap between them.

"Don't say anything," she whispered.

He looked surprised as she pulled him tight against her and then paused as she looked deep into his eyes.

The moment she looked into those blue eyes, she knew she had made a huge mistake, and it was probably because she was completely exhausted and really hadn't thought it through. All she had been thinking about was Matthew and their first night together ten years ago.

She hadn't looked at him closely enough, and she felt foolish.

She let go of him and took a step back.

"You're not Matthew." She sighed, annoyed with herself for her mistake.

Again.

Marcus grinned, his eyes twinkling. "No, but I could be if you'd like!"

* * *

Why hadn't Victoria said she wanted to stay here?

He was offering her a chance to remain in St. Thomas. He couldn't actually offer her a job unless it was okayed by the board of directors, but he didn't want her to go. It hurt him that New York City came first. It always did.

He wanted her to think beyond Manhattan.

Even though he'd vowed he wouldn't put his heart at risk with her again, he still wanted her, even after all this time. And he wanted her here.

With him.

Only she wanted New York, it was clear. Why had he thought she would change after all this time?

Ever since their trip to his parents' place on St. Croix, when she had come out of the pool house in that white bikini, he hadn't been able to stop thinking about her. And then when they were swimming up to the edge, it had taken all his willpower not to kiss her.

And for the past week, even though they had been completely stressed and focused on getting this domino back up and running, all he could think about was her in that bikini.

Which then drifted to his memories of her naked and in his arms…

"Why are you looking at me like that?" she whispered huskily.

He was propped up on one elbow and running his fingers through her brown hair as they were lying in an on-call room, crammed into one small bed.

"How am I looking at you?"

She grinned. "I don't know."

"You're beautiful."

"You're crazy," she said.

"I know."

And he wanted to tell her that he was crazy for her, but he didn't want to scare her off.

"Hey, do you have a minute?"

Matthew turned to see Marcus in the doorway to his office and groaned inwardly. Of course Marcus had to intrude on his thoughts now. Memories that he wanted to savor but now were melting away in the presence of his twin.

"Now is not a good time, Marcus. I'm trying to find another donor."

"I'm not here to bug you." Marcus shut the door behind him. "I have good news."

"Oh? You have three kidneys, so you're giving up two?" Matthew teased.

Marcus grinned. "You know if I did, I would."

"I know," Matthew admitted.

Marcus raised his eyebrow. "Wow."

"What?" Matthew asked.

"You've never admitted that I've been right before."

"Marcus, I don't have the patience for this today." He rubbed his temples. "What is your news?"

"I've found a donor, and they are getting cross matched and ready to go through counseling."

"Who?"

"A friend of Jonas's is donating in the surgery. By the way, I would've still given my kidney to Mrs. Van Luven. I thought I would put that out there. I wouldn't have left your patient in the lurch."

Matthew sighed. "Well, that is good news. I hope that the cross match works for Jonas."

"Me, too. There's also something else."

"What?" Matthew asked.

"What're your intentions with Victoria?"

Matthew's spine straightened. He didn't like where this was heading. Marcus was a lothario. Had never had a serious relationship. He was a playboy through and through, and the thought of Marcus setting his sights on Victoria made his blood boil. “What do you mean?”

“She pulled me into her arms and was going to kiss me…and then she realized I wasn’t you.”

Matthew’s pulse thundered between his ears. “She what?”

“She almost kissed me.” Marcus grinned. “I was kind of hopeful, but she pulled away pretty quickly once she realized that I wasn’t you. She’s into you, so my question is, what’re you going to do about it?”

“Nothing.” Even though his heart was racing and he couldn’t help but smile.

Victoria wanted to kiss him, but he wasn’t going to admit to his brother that he wanted Victoria, too. His brother didn’t even know the details of their shared past. No one knew about that. It was his alone.

He didn’t like Marcus questioning him about it. It was too intrusive.

“What do you mean, you’re not going to do anything?” Marcus asked in shock. “She’s obviously into you.”

"So?" He acted like he didn't care even though it gave him a secret thrill.

"So? Kirsten has been gone for five years, Matthew. She wouldn't want you to be alone."

"Don't talk to me about Kirsten," Matthew snarled.

"Why?" Marcus asked. "You're unbelievable. If I were you—"

"But you're not me."

"Thank goodness for that! You're too uptight. Though heck knows Mom and Dad always wanted me to be more like you. You act more like a parent than a brother. I'd rather have a brother!"

Matthew crossed his arms. "What are we doing, Marcus? Why are you suddenly so concerned with my love life?"

Marcus shrugged. "I honestly don't know, but I thought you'd want to know this. And I know that you two knew each other in the past, but I think more happened than you're letting on."

Matthew didn't say anything, so Marcus left his office, slamming the door behind him. He felt bad, but he didn't want Marcus to know about his past with Victoria.

Why?

He couldn't answer that niggling little voice inside his head.

Marcus wanted a brother.

He wanted that, too.

And he wanted Victoria.

What was holding him back?

She wanted him.

That gave him a secret thrill.

Why was he fighting that old attraction?

It was his fault just as much as hers when things crashed and burned ten years ago. He'd left her and New York, after all. He could've stayed. They had both grown and moved on.

Why couldn't they just have one more night?

Does she even want one more night?

He wasn't sure, but he would take one more night with her, if he could. He was scared of being hurt again. He didn't have much luck when it came to love.

There were no happily-ever-afters for him.

Of course there won't be if you don't try.

He left his office and made his way back to the boardroom. Victoria was pacing back and forth. She was mumbling to herself, and she looked annoyed.

He knocked on the door.

She paused, her cheeks turning red, and she took a step back. "Matthew?"

"Yes."

"Do you know how frustrating it is that you're an identical twin! Did Marcus tell you what happened?"

Matthew chuckled softly. "He did."

"He promised me he'd grow a beard," Victoria groused. "So I could tell you two apart faster."

"So why did you pull him into that embrace?"

The red deepened to crimson. "I wasn't thinking straight."

"Obviously. I'm much more dashing than my brother." He grinned.

"Stubborn is more like it," she said, smiling.

"He says uptight." Matthew laughed. "It's okay that you mistook him for me. I get it. Twin thing."

"Well, okay. Thank you. Again, I'm sorry, but Marcus did have good news. Did he tell you about it?"

Matthew nodded. "Yes. Now we just have to wait to make sure that the cross match is good."

"My fingers are crossed." And she held them up.

"Well, there's nothing more we can do here today. Do you want to get dinner?"

She froze. "Do you think that's wise?"

"Why wouldn't it be?" he asked, confused.

"Because of what happened that first time we had dinner."

He took a step closer to her and touched her face. "I'm okay with what happened last time. Victoria, I like being with you, and I think it's safe for us to have dinner together while we wait for the news. How about I cook you dinner?"

"You can cook?" she asked, surprised.

"I can. So what do you think?"

She worried at her bottom lip and then nodded. "That sounds like a plan."

"I'll send you my address. I'm going to leave a bit early today."

"Why?" she asked.

"I have to buy some groceries to actually make you dinner. Unless you have affinity for warm beer and a half bag of crackers."

She chuckled. "Send me your address and the time you want me there."

"I will. Try not to stress about the domino. Have faith."

"No promises."

Matthew nodded and left the room.

He wasn't sure what he was doing, but he was going to take a chance.

It didn't have to mean anything other than two friends getting together.

That was it.

His heart didn't have to get involved—even though he was pretty sure that his heart was already in serious danger.

CHAPTER TEN

THE CAB DROPPED her off at the bottom of Matthew's hilly driveway. Thankfully it wasn't long, and she walked up the hill to a white stucco-walled house with a red roof. It was cute and modest. It was completely different than the house he'd grown up in.

As in, it wasn't a castle. It wasn't a showpiece.

It blended in with Charlotte Amalie like it belonged, and you wouldn't even really notice it was there unless you looked for it.

It really suited him. He might have called himself uptight, but she didn't see that side of Matthew. Or maybe it was that she was the one who was the most rigid and he seemed mellow in comparison.

That thought made her smile.

Matthew's home kind of reminded her of the pool house on St. Croix. It was red and white against the lush green that grew up the volcanically formed island. The roof was a bright cherry red that stuck out from the green that climbed and grew around it.

After Matthew had suggested they have dinner, she'd gone straight back to her place and changed out of her work clothes and into a flowing black dress that she had bought in the local marketplace.

The air was so humid, and she needed something breezy tonight. Something she could feel comfortable in. And she needed to feel comfortable. Something was in the air, and she was a bundle of nerves.

She wasn't sure what or if anything would happen, but at least she wouldn't be dying of heat in her work clothes.

She knocked on the door, and Matthew answered it.

"Hi," he greeted her. "Come on in."

She stepped inside and was shocked at the inside of his home. From the outside it looked like a small house built onto the side of the hill, like all the other homes in the neighborhood.

It was like an optical illusion. Tiny on the outside, large and spacious on the inside.

"This is beautiful and so deceptive."

"Deceptive? That's a word I've never heard to describe my house before."

She chuckled. "What I mean was I wasn't expecting it to be so big!"

He waggled his eyebrows. "Well..."

Victoria groaned and then laughed at his joke. "Ugh, you know what I mean."

"I do, but I can have some fun, can't I?" His eyes were twinkling, and she had butterflies in her stomach. This was the Matthew she remembered from the first time she'd met him.

"You sound like your brother when you say stuff like that."

Matthew winced. "Like a dagger to my heart."

"Oh, stop. Really, though, this is gorgeous and not what I expected."

Matthew smiled. "It's built up the hillside. It was a wreck when I bought it, but it helped with my grief. Work at the hospital during the day, renovating at night."

"You bought this place after your wife died?"

He nodded. "We had a small condo and it reminded me of her pain and her suffering. I couldn't stay there."

"I get that."

"We're really getting into a depressing subject, aren't we?"

She laughed nervously. "Yes. It's been stressful enough recently, and I really don't want to add to it while we wait to see if the new donor is viable."

"Agreed. Let's have dinner al fresco tonight," Matthew suggested.

"That sounds great."

Even though it was humid, there was a nice breeze as the sun was setting. Matthew's house was modern and open. It was a blend of contemporary and that old Caribbean vibe.

Dark wood and white.

She followed him through an open set of French doors out onto a secluded patio surrounded by green fronds, flowers and vines, intermixed with twinkle lights. Almost like a secret garden that was tucked away.

"Not as stunning as a sea view on a mountain, but it's a quiet retreat in the city."

As if he had to explain. If she had to choose in this moment, she would pick his home, tucked away in the city, over the castle on the hill on St. Croix.

"It's beautiful," she murmured. There was a trickling, bubbling sound of water from a fountain. It was perfect.

"I do have a sea-slash-city view from my room, but sometimes you just need a quiet place to think. If you follow those stairs down, I also have a small private beach."

"A private beach sounds wonderful."

"It's really peaceful."

"Yes," she sighed. "I could do with that tonight."

Matthew pulled out her chair and she sat down.

"Would you like some wine? Nonalcoholic, of course, just in case we get a call!"

"Yes, please."

He poured her a glass of sparkling white and sat down across from her.

"Do you have your phone on?" he asked.

"I do. Not that I can rush into surgery tonight if it was a match, no matter how much I want to. Everyone needs to be present and ready to make it work, but as soon as we have a kidney, I'll start calling everyone in to get it started."

"Marcus is more than ready," Matthew mumbled.

"I know. He's made a lot of this possible."

A strange look crossed his face. "Marcus likes you, you know."

"What?" she asked, laughing nervously.

"He told me," he stated firmly.

Heat unfurled in her belly. Was he jealous?

"I like Marcus, too, but not in that way. As soon as I knew he wasn't you, I stepped away from him."

"Really?" he asked. "Why? Most women like him."

"He's not the brother I cared for." Her pulse was pounding between her ears, and she was trembling.

Had she really just said that?

Even when they were together in New York, she had never really told him how she felt about him. She'd never told Mathew that she cared for him.

That she loved him.

That she thought she still might.

It killed her that she did, because nothing could come from it. She could put her heart on the line, but she wouldn't risk his.

Her life was in New York. It was not here in St. Thomas.

Why can't it be?

She shook that thought away. She wasn't going to follow a man or put her heart on the line, no matter how much she wanted to.

And she did want to.

He gazed at her, his eyes mesmerizing her,

and she was frozen, unable to move—not that she wanted to.

She yearned for him.

Even after all this time, she wanted him. Nothing had changed.

"He said you're interested in me and I should go for it," he whispered.

"Should you?" she asked, breathlessly.

"Should I?"

Her breath quickened, and she laughed nervously. "So I suppose he knows about our past, then?"

"No."

"No?"

"What we had, what we shared, isn't anyone else's business. It's my memories, and he doesn't deserve to know. I don't want to share that with him."

It was getting harder to breathe. "So what did you tell him?"

A smile tugged at the corner of his lips. "Nothing."

"I see."

"Why did you want to kiss me?" he asked softly, his voice husky and full of a promise she wanted desperately to indulge in.

She wanted to be with him.

He stood and knelt in front of her. "I've

wanted to kiss you every day since you first arrived back here."

"Have you?" Her voice caught in her throat.

He nodded. "You broke me when you ended things."

Her heart shattered, knowing that she had hurt him. She had known he was angry, but she hadn't realized he was actually hurt by it. She'd beens hurt, too, when he left and didn't fight for her, but it was her choice to stay and take that job, so she didn't feel like she had the right to be angry.

"I never wanted to hurt you. I thought you were mad and I thought it was about the position in New York."

"It was never about that," he said.

"You know that's all that mattered to me. I told you that right from the beginning."

"I know, but I couldn't help it. I fell for you. For so long after it ended, I was mad. I didn't understand why you chose the job over me, but I understand why now."

Tears stung her eyes. "I never wanted to make you feel that way. Against my better judgment, I cared for you. I don't think I've ever stopped."

"You've haunted my soul for ten years."

She swallowed the lump in her throat. She

reached out and touched his face. "I've never stopped thinking about you, either, Matthew. And I think you know why I wanted to kiss you. I have missed you, but I need you to know that I'm going back to New York when this is all over. That hasn't changed. My life is there, and I don't want to hurt you again."

He nodded. "I know, and I don't want anything more. I just want one more night with you. One more night to lay the ghost of us to rest."

She bent over and kissed him. A light kiss as she trembled with anticipation.

She didn't know what she was doing. All she knew was she wanted him.

Even if was it was just temporary. Maybe he was right and this last time would be closure.

As he said, it was laying the ghost of them to rest.

She wanted tonight.

She wanted to be with him again.

His hands slipped into her hair as the kiss deepened, and she melted into the hot desire that had been bubbling under the surface for years. Matthew was all she'd ever wanted, and she had always been too scared to reach out and take him.

She'd ruined it, but she could have this with him. One more moment of absolute pleasure.

His hands moved down her back, and he broke the kiss only for a moment to effortlessly scoop her up into his arms and carry her into his house. It was a few stairs up to the loft bedroom, and a zing of excitement went through her as she spied the large four-poster mahogany bed. The kind she'd pictured making love to him in.

He set her down, and she ran her hands over him, slipping her fingers under his shirt to touch him and reveling in the feel of goose bumps on his skin as she traced her fingers over his flat stomach.

"Are you sure you truly want this, Victoria?" he asked, leaning his forehead against hers, his arms around her.

"Yes. As long as you have protection, then yes, I want this, Matthew."

I've missed you.

Yet she couldn't bring herself to say those words out loud. She kept them locked away inside. She was still too afraid to tell him, to risk her heart.

But she could have this.

"Yes. I have protection."

"And you want me, too?" she asked, kissing his neck.

He chuckled. "I do."

He cupped her face, kissing her again as she unbuttoned his shirt.

She wanted nothing between them. She just wanted them together. Skin to skin.

For one night she'd feel safe again, with his arms around her.

His hands trailed over her body, touching her, and she responded, even though the light silk of her dress separated them. Her nipples puckered as he cupped her breast. Her body was quivering with desire.

He undid her dress, pushing it over her shoulders. It pooled at her feet. She was naked save her black lace underwear.

"Victoria," he murmured as he brushed her hair to the side and kissed her neck, running his hands over her exposed skin.

She shivered in delight.

There was no turning back now. Not that she wanted to.

This was what she had dreamed about in her darkest hours for the last ten years when she was alone, missing him.

She pulled off his shirt, baring his sun-bronzed chest, and then worked on his belt.

He sucked in his breath and gripped her wrists, pushing her against the mattress.

She cried out in delight, and he grinned as he moved over her and kissed her.

His kisses trailed from her mouth then down over her body to her breasts, his tongue igniting her blood as he captured one of her nipples with a kiss.

She cried out.

"Protection," she murmured, reminding him again.

He grinned lazily. "Right."

He moved and pulled a condom out of the nightstand drawer.

She sat up. "Let me."

Matthew moaned as she rolled the condom over him. She liked touching him, teasing him the same way he'd teased her.

"You're torturing me," he murmured.

She laughed. "I know."

He pushed her back down, slipping off her underwear, and this time his kisses trailed lower and she cried out when his tongue touched her between her legs. Her body burned for him to fill her.

To take her.

She arched against his mouth.

"Please," she whispered.

"As you wish." Matthew settled between her thighs, and their gazes locked as he entered her. She moaned as he filled her, her legs locking around his hips, not wanting to let him go. He moved so slowly, gently, taking his time when all she wanted was fast.

Hard.

She wanted him to take her.

It had been so long and she was hungry for him. He quickened his pace in response to her hips urging him to take her like she wanted. Pleasure began to unfurl in the pit of her stomach, and she tightened her hold on his back, her nails digging into his skin.

She cried out as heady pleasure washed through her.

Even though she wanted it this way, she wanted it to last forever.

She didn't want this to end.

Matthew came soon after her, resting against her as he caught his breath. He rolled away, but he pulled her with him, not letting her go as he held her.

Victoria clung to him, not wanting this to end as she listened to the comforting sound of his heart.

Her eyes were stinging, full of tears that she wouldn't shed. She couldn't let them come.

She couldn't risk her heart or his.

So she swallowed the tears down.

Instead, she just reveled in this moment with the man she now knew she had always loved.

The man she wouldn't—couldn't—ever let herself have.

CHAPTER ELEVEN

MATTHEW COULDN'T QUITE believe that had happened. He'd dreamed about this happening again for so long, but he was never sure that it would.

He'd thought Victoria was his past, never his future.

She still isn't. Don't get attached.

He'd dreamed about it happening so many times over the years, because he missed her, but he hadn't thought that he would ever see her again.

He'd made his peace with that and moved on.

Then he'd lost his wife.

And he was left alone, with just the memories of the two women he'd loved more than anything haunting him.

It was like some kind of dream when she told him that she still wanted him. And it was a dream that he didn't want to end, even though he knew it was going to.

She had told him that it would.

She was going back to New York.

At least this time he would be prepared for it. He wouldn't be blindsided, and he wouldn't be hurt when she left.

Liar.

His heart wanted more, even though he couldn't have more. He was angry with himself for falling for her again. For setting himself up for more pain.

She rested her chin on her fists and stared at him. Those deep brown eyes were so mesmerizing, and all his anger at himself melted away. All that mattered was being with her in this moment.

"What?" he asked, still touching her back as they lay there in the dark.

"Did you actually cook dinner or was it all a ruse to get me into bed?" she teased.

Her little joke broke the tension, the anxiety he was feeling in those fleeting moments.

He laughed. "I did plan a light dinner, but I hadn't started cooking it yet. Maybe a part of me was subconsciously hoping this would happen."

Victoria grinned. “I’m glad that it did.”

“Me, too. Shall we try and make something of dinner?” he asked, even though he didn’t want to get out of bed. He wanted to stay here forever with her.

“That sounds good.” She got up and he watched her, his body stirring with desire as she padded across the room and pulled on her clothing. She tied back her long, soft hair.

He got up and sneaked up behind her, wrapping his arms around her to kiss her slender neck.

“I thought you were hungry?” she asked.

“I am, but not for food.” And he kissed her neck again.

“Stop.” She laughed, pushing him away, but he wasn’t so easily put off.

He wanted her again.

They had said only one night, and the night was not over.

He pulled off her dress and pushed her against the wall, kissing her, touching her.

The phone rang then, like a shrill harpy, and he groaned, annoyed by whoever was disrupting him.

“It could be about the surgery,” she reminded him, but there was disappointment in her voice.

"Why are they calling me, then?" he grumbled.

She pulled her phone out of her purse. "My phone's dead."

"Fine. I'll answer," he groused.

"You really have no choice."

He nodded and let her go. He pulled on his trousers and made his way downstairs to answer the phone.

"Dr. Olesen speaking."

"Hi, Dr. Olesen, it's Dr. Gainsbourg. I was trying to call Dr. Jensen, but she's not answering."

"It's okay. Her phone is dead. What do you need, Dr. Gainsbourg?"

"The new donor has been approved and cleared."

"Great." Matthew gave Victoria thumbs-up, and she mouthed a silent thank-you to the ceiling.

"Mrs. Van Luven and Jonas Fredrick have both taken a turn for the worse, so we need to prep them for surgery. The domino needs to happen now."

Matthew's heart sank. "I see."

"Do you want me to call the others in? We

have two donors and three recipients here already in Charlotte Amalie."

"I'll pass you over to Dr. Jensen. It's her surgery." Matthew handed her the phone.

"What's going on?" Victoria asked, and he watched her face, but it was unreadable.

Calm.

Collected.

A true surgeon.

And he couldn't help but admire her. He loved her. He always had. He just couldn't have her.

His life was here, and hers was in New York. She would leave him again.

Maybe they won't want her back?

That idea thrilled him, but it was hard to believe. She was an excellent surgeon. It was why she'd earned that coveted position ten years ago. The autopsy findings had cleared her of any fault, so the press would soon move on from what had happened and no one would care anymore.

Her life could go back to normal.

"Get them all in and schedule the operating rooms as early as you can." Victoria hung up and worried her bottom lip.

"So we're doing the domino?" he asked.

She nodded. "First we eat. We need food."

He grinned. "And then straight to the hospital to start prepping."

Victoria smiled. "Marcus has already admitted himself."

Matthew rolled his eyes at the impertinence of his brother, but something else struck him. The stark reality that his brother could die.

That his twin was putting his life on the line for another.

He shook that thought away. "Eager, isn't he?"

"Are you ready?" Victoria asked.

"As long as you handle Marcus's harvest, I can work on Mrs. Van Luven."

She nodded. "This will work. Your staff are ready."

"I know." He took her in his arms, even though he knew he should keep his distance. Her month was almost up. She'd soon be gone from his life. "Thank you for helping me. Thank you for coming here and organizing this."

"I didn't have a choice. Remember?" she murmured.

"I know, but I'm glad it's you here." He let her go, even though he didn't want to.

It felt like she was already slipping away. Like his dream was melting with the dawn.

"Go have a shower. I'll get dinner ready," he said.

She nodded and headed to the bathroom.

Matthew sighed and started the coffee machine, because he had a feeling they were going to need it.

After a quick bite to eat where they talked of nothing but the procedure, they headed to the hospital and were there in time to get the first arrivals admitted. All the other elective surgeries had been postponed and the surgical floor was mobilized, primed and ready for the procedure.

They arrived at the hospital at three in the morning, and the first surgery was slated for six.

There was a buzz of anxiety and excitement in the air. A few of the local newspapers had started sending reporters as news got out the domino was about to take place.

Ziese Memorial Hospital was a new hospital in Charlotte Amalie, and this surgery was a first for the hospital. There was also the fact that Dr. Victoria Jensen was the lead surgeon.

Matthew had been expecting it. He was worried it would affect Victoria, but the attention didn't seem to faze her.

A whiteboard in the unit laid out the procedure so that all staff could see where each patient was going and which surgeon was involved. Six donors and six recipients. Matthew's stomach did a flip-flop to see Marcus's name up there on the board.

He was up first.

He's a grown man.

But he couldn't help but be worried about his twin as he stared at Marcus's picture.

What would he do if he lost him? He'd never really thought about it before, and it was an unwelcome thought that made him sick to his stomach.

When Marcus had said he wanted a brother, Matthew realized he wanted a brother, too. Only he hadn't said that, and if Marcus died, he would lose the chance to tell him.

He would lose someone else he cared about.

"It'll be okay," Victoria said from where she was standing beside him, as if sensing his apprehension.

Only a few hours ago, they had been wrapped up in each other's arms. Now they were standing on the precipice of a historical surgery. A complicated surgery that relied on so many moving parts.

"I'm glad you're handling Marcus and

Jonas," he said. And he was. There was no one else he would trust more.

"And I'm glad you've got Mrs. Van Luven. I wouldn't trust anyone else but you with her," she said. "You're my right-hand surgeon."

"Thanks."

"Have you gone to see Marcus?" she asked.

"No." He swallowed the lump in his throat.

"You should. He'll need support after this is done. You're his family."

"Hardly. He's never really needed me."

And when have you needed him?

Matthew was keenly aware of how many times he'd pushed Marcus away…

"I can help," Marcus said. "We can talk. I'm here."

"Talk about what?" Matthew snapped.

"You're grieving."

"Don't. You know nothing about my pain. You know nothing about heartache. You bounce from woman to woman. What do you know of love?"

Marcus frowned. "Fine. You don't need me. I get it. I don't need you, either, but you're wrong about me."

"Am I?" Matthew asked.

"Yes. I've known heartache. I've known

grief. But it's obvious you don't care, because you notice nothing around you. Just yourself."

After that Marcus had pushed him away for good, made it clear he didn't need Matthew.

Just like Victoria didn't really need him.

Go, a little voice told him. Only he couldn't. He was too ashamed of his stubbornness.

Victoria looked at him, unsure. "Are you sure you don't want to go see him? I'm about to wheel him into surgery."

"I'm sure. He's a grown man, and he won't want to see me before he goes under the knife."

There was a part of him worried for his twin.

This was major surgery.

Marcus was doing something very unselfish for what, Matthew felt, was the first time in his life. Matthew had spent so many years trying to look out for Marcus, thinking his brother couldn't take care of himself.

Clearly he'd been wrong.

No wonder Marcus didn't want to be around him.

He wasn't a very good brother or a very good friend.

Right now, though, he had to focus on saving a life. Marcus was in good hands. He had to focus on Mrs. Van Luven.

Victoria wanted to do the laparoscopic approach, which was a longer surgery than the open procedure but would be better for recovery. Although open surgery was always an option if things went bad.

Matthew's heart sank.

He hoped things didn't go bad.

Marcus was wheeled into the operating room just as Victoria was getting her gown on and the scrub nurses prepped the surgical field.

She knew Matthew was in the next operating room prepping Mrs. Van Luven to receive Marcus's kidney, and he was putting all his trust in her to take care of his twin brother. She was shocked he hadn't wanted to see Marcus first, but Matthew was stubborn.

Victoria hoped Marcus had that same stubborn streak. It would help him during recovery.

Once she had Marcus's kidney out, it would go to Mrs. Van Luven, and then the next donor would be wheeled in.

Each step was precise in its movement.

It would be a long, grueling day as this multistep surgery was performed.

As she stepped into the operating room, she did what she knew Matthew always did—something she never did—and that was to take in a deep breath and breathe in the energy.

The life that swirled through these hallowed halls. The life on the table that was in her hands.

"Vic, are you here yet?" There was a hint of nervousness in Marcus's voice.

"I'm here," Victoria responded. As she approached the surgical table, she saw there was fear in his eyes, those eyes that were so similar to Matthew's, but also different. She smiled at him, even though he couldn't see it behind her surgical mask. "I thought Matthew told you I didn't like being called Vic."

He grinned. "I'm sorry. I'm nervous. Doctors can be anxious, too."

"It's okay. I don't care if you call me Vic. Actually, I like it from you."

"You do?" he asked.

"Yes, because it's you. And I like you, Marcus."

He smiled. "I knew I'd like you, too, Vic. Just make sure my pigheaded brother knows it's okay I can call you that. I don't need him on my case."

"I promise. He does care about you. He doesn't mean to always be on your case."

Marcus snorted—just like Matthew did, she noticed—then he frowned. "There's a lot of press out there."

"I know," she said dryly.

"I know why. I read your story."

Her heart skipped a beat, her blood running cold. "You shouldn't worry about that."

"I'm not," Marcus said. "I know that was beyond your control. I know you're an excellent surgeon. It's why my brother loves you."

She swallowed a lump in her throat, trying not to react to what he was saying. "They start painkillers early here, I see."

She was trying to deflect from the truth.

He grinned. "I trust you, Vic. I'm in good hands."

"Thanks."

The anesthesiologist took over then, and Marcus was put under.

Victoria took a deep, calming breath as she stared at the surgical field.

You've got this. You've done this before.

She was a good surgeon.

The ambassador's surgery might have

had a sad outcome, but she had never once doubted her surgical abilities.

She knew who she was and what she was capable of.

This was Matthew's twin, and she was going to keep him safe and make sure this gift he was giving was put to good use in saving a life.

"Scalpel."

The scrub nurse handed her what she needed as Victoria drowned out everything else.

She knew this surgery well.

She'd done it numerous times before. That was why she was the best transplant surgeon in New York. That was why the ambassador had come to her hospital and wanted her, and as she worked she thought about all the lives that would be saved because this domino was taking place.

All the happy families that wouldn't lose a loved one.

Not that she knew anything about that, but she got a high from saving lives. This was why she'd wanted to be a surgeon. It wasn't the money.

It wasn't the business.

It was helping people.

Marcus's kidney was beautiful and healthy.

She removed it and placed it on ice, dousing it with preservation solution as she closed up the artery.

It was then that history came to bite her in the butt one more time as fate decided that this was the moment to test her. The monitors tracking Marcus's vitals sounded the alarm.

"His sats are dropping. Blood pressure is low," the anesthesiologist stated.

Her pulse thundered between her ears as the artery began to bulge and bleed. There was a clot.

"Come on, Marcus. A clot. Really?"

The urgent beeping of the monitors echoed in her head, but this time she refused to freeze up. This was Matthew's twin. She wasn't going to let him die.

The flat-line echo dissipated, and she continued her work, finding the clot and evacuating it. The bleeding slowed, and monitor's alarms ceased.

"Blood pressure is rising to normal. The patient is stable."

"Good." Her voice shook as she finished the repair. Her whole body apart from her hands shook, but she didn't have time to give in to that anxious energy.

Marcus was stable, and she had a kidney to deliver.

"Dr. Gainsbourg, please finish up here," she said, hoping her voice didn't shake.

"Yes, Dr. Jensen."

Marcus was doing well now, and she had to prep for the next surgery. She wanted to bring Mrs. Van Luven's new kidney to Matthew and let him know that Marcus was okay. She might not understand their sibling dynamic, but she wanted him to know that everything was fine. His brother would recover.

She carried the kidney into the next operating room, where Matthew was working over Mrs. Van Luven.

Matthew looked up as she came in.

"I was expecting you sooner," he said.

"There was a complication."

Matthew's eyes widened. "What?"

"A clot at the suture line. It's fine now, though."

"He's okay then?" he asked, and she could hear the fear in his voice.

"He's excellent. Is Mrs. Van Luven ready for her new kidney?"

"More than ready," Matthew responded.

Victoria handed the kidney off to the resident assisting Matthew. She then stayed to watch, as she had some time before the next procedure because Jonas's donor had only just been taken into the theater.

She watched as Matthew gently lifted his brother's kidney and grafted it into Mrs. Van Luven's body. She leaned over, watching with trepidation as they waited for the pink color to return to the kidney as Matthew finished suturing it into place and removed the clamp.

Victoria held her breath as Matthew nudged the kidney with his finger. Pink flooded the organ as blood began to flow, and there was a small spout of urine, which was a good sign.

"Excellent work, Dr. Olesen."

"Thank you, Dr. Jensen." Matthew smiled, and she felt relief.

Victoria left the operating room.

Her day of surgery had only just begun, but this was a great start to a long day.

An excellent start in her books.

And things were looking brighter than she'd thought they would.

When Matthew finished with Mrs. Van Luven, he went on to the next procedure, even though all he'd wanted to do since Victoria had told him about the clot was to rush to the intensive care unit and check on Marcus. His life with his brother flashed before his eyes, and he regretted all those years they'd wasted fighting.

Marcus was stable, and Matthew knew his brother would kill him if he didn't stay and finish the domino.

And he couldn't let his team down.

He wouldn't let Victoria down.

It was a long day, and he was out of the practice of doing back-to-back surgeries, but he wouldn't be anywhere else. This was where he belonged, working alongside Victoria.

Except she doesn't want to stay.

The world would know soon this domino had been a success, and she'd leave. She'd made it quite clear that when New York called, she'd be gone.

The donors were stable in the postoperative care unit, and he had heard that Marcus had been taken to his own room.

Matthew stretched his back and wandered the halls looking for Victoria, but he couldn't find her, and he had to go speak to the press about the surgery soon.

Eventually he found her in the doctors' lounge. She was leaning against a wall with her eyes closed, and she looked exhausted.

"There you are," he said, his heart melting. She'd done so well today. So many lives saved. He wished she would stay for their hospital. He wished she would stay for him.

Only he couldn't ask her to do that.

She opened one eye and looked at him. "If you're looking for your usual celebratory sex session, keep moving. I need sleep."

He chuckled. "The thought had crossed my mind."

She smiled weakly. "How is everyone?"

"Stable. Doing well. Including Marcus."

"Have you gone to see him?" she asked wearily.

"No. I will soon, though."

"Good."

"The press wants to speak with us."

Victoria groaned. "Of course they do."

"I could speak to them alone so that you can go and sleep?"

"Would you mind?" she asked.

He shook his head. "No. Not at all. I'm the chief of surgery—this is my usual job."

"I would, but I just don't want questions about the ambassador. I told them what happened, but that doesn't seem to matter to the press. I don't want anything to do with them."

"Go. Sleep. I've got this."

She nodded. "I'm headed to an on-call

room, so that's where you can find me if needed. I'm not leaving here until everyone is out of the intensive care unit."

Victoria shuffled off to an on-call room, and Matthew made his way to the hospital media room.

The press would be disappointed. He knew it was her they wanted to speak to, and only because of what had happened in New York, but he didn't want the world to focus on what she had done in the past. He wanted them to focus on the good she'd done today.

Maybe you need to let go of the past, too?

He shook that niggling thought away as he straightened his white lab coat and headed into a room of reporters.

CHAPTER TWELVE

VICTORIA TRIED TO SLEEP, but her phone kept pinging, and finally she was forced to give up and opened her email instead. There were messages from Paul and the board of directors at the hospital saying she'd been cleared to come back and take up her practice again. Which annoyed her. Was it only because she'd "redeemed" herself with the domino that they wanted her back?

They weren't begging her to return when the autopsy had first cleared her.

Not that she would've abandoned the domino.

It was almost like the board had been waiting to see how this surgery played out.

It felt like they weren't really on her side.

It made her angry.

Going back to New York City was everything she'd wanted since she first came to St. Thomas.

So why was Matthew the only thing she could think about now?

Maybe because he had faith in you all along.

Matthew was the type of guy who wanted forever, and she wasn't sure she could ever give anyone that.

You could if you weren't so afraid.

And she was.

She was terrified of relying on someone else or having someone rely on her. She didn't want to let him down. She wouldn't hurt anyone if it was only her. She would only have to worry about herself, and if she died she wouldn't leave anyone behind. No one would have to mourn her.

Miss her.

There would be no children who could be lost in the foster system the way she'd been. Even if part of her wanted that family.

A home.

She wanted it all, but she was terrified of losing it if she took the chance. She was terrified Matthew would leave her.

He'd left her once before.

She set her phone down and curled up on

her side, trying to sleep. She couldn't, even though she was bone weary.

In the dark of the small on-call room, she felt like she was that frightened kid again.

Alone.

No one to love her and yearning for a family.

She'd broken Matthew's heart ten years ago. If he did love her, she'd ruined it then, but she was glad they were still friends.

She didn't need any more than that.

Liar.

Except she did.

There was a knock at the door, and Matthew peeked his head in the room.

"You awake?" he asked.

"Yeah. I couldn't sleep," she said.

Which wasn't a lie. She couldn't. All she could think about was having to leave Matthew, how she'd ruined things ten years ago, and there was a part of her that was wondering how her life would've been different had she chosen another path. If she'd chosen love over her career. How much had been wasted because of her fear of the unknown?

"Press conference is over. The world knows you are a success again."

"Thanks." And she meant it.

Matthew always seemed to come to her rescue.

She didn't deserve a guy like him.

He came in and shut the door. "I checked on Mrs. Van Luven."

"Oh?"

"She's putting out yellow urine and her creatinine is the best I've seen it since she was admitted."

A thrill surged through her. "That's wonderful."

"I thought that would please you. Her family is ecstatic."

A lump formed in her throat. Mrs. Van Luven had a family waiting for her. Every single one of her recipients and donors had someone that cared for them, because even though Matthew didn't want to admit it, he cared for his brother, Marcus.

If it was her, she would have no one to lean on.

She never had anyone to lean on.

You have Matthew.

Except she didn't. She couldn't stay here and risk her heart.

She had to go back to New York City.

She was glad for her patients, though. Their

lives were saved, their families made whole, and that's why she was a surgeon.

She might be alone, but she saved lives.

"I'm glad they're happy." She patted the spot on the bed next to her. She wanted him to join her. Though she shouldn't tempt fate, she wanted him again. To forget her loneliness, the sadness that her time here was almost over.

She wanted to make love with Matthew one last time before she headed back to New York City and her empty, lonely life.

Before the phone had rung, before the surgery, they had been headed back to bed, and just thinking about his hands on her, his mouth kissing her everywhere, fired her senses.

Tonight, she wanted him one more time.

Matthew sat down next to her, and she leaned against him. He stroked her back.

"Thank you for all your help," she whispered.

"You were amazing. You're such a talented surgeon. I'm in awe of you." He touched her face, and her body trembled under his gentle caress.

"I still couldn't have done it without you."

You're my everything.

Only she couldn't say that out loud. So instead she kissed him, putting all the things she couldn't say into that kiss.

"Victoria," he murmured against her lips.

"I need you, Matthew."

And she did. Not just for this night. She wanted him always, but she was too scared to take a chance and grab forever.

Matthew stood and locked the door, peeling off his white lab coat as she pulled off her scrubs. She wanted hot and heavy tonight.

Her body trembled with need, her pulse racing with anticipation, knowing what was to come.

She was ready for him.

Her body craved him, and even though she shouldn't do this, she tried to tell herself this would be the perfect goodbye. As he'd said before, a way to lay the ghost of them to rest.

Or wake the beast.

It didn't take long to get out of their scrubs, and soon she was in his arms, his lips on hers as he pressed her against the wall.

"Dammit," he cursed.

"What?"

"I don't have protection."

"It's okay. I'm on birth control." She was, and she didn't want to him to stop. She preferred to have both the pill and a condom, but this time she'd just take him.

She wanted to feel all of him.

She needed him.

"Are you sure?" he asked.

"Positive."

His hand slipped between them as he pressed her against the wall. He was touching her, causing zings of heady pleasure to zip through her body. She reached down to touch him. He was hard and ready for her.

Matthew hefted her up, and she wrapped her legs around his waist as he thrust into her.

"Why do I want you?" he moaned against her neck. "You consume my every thought."

"I want you, too," she murmured against his lips as he thrust into her again.

She wanted to tell him how she felt. She wanted Matthew to know that she loved him and that she had always loved him.

She couldn't form the words, so she reveled in the feeling of him taking her the way she'd always wanted.

"Victoria, you feel so good," he moaned.

"Don't stop," she cried, holding on to him.

She was weak when it came to him. She always had been. Victoria though she was strong, but she wasn't. The tears stung her eyes again, and she didn't want to cry.

Not now.

Not with him buried inside her.

She came quickly, and he followed her. Her body felt boneless.

The tears started flowing then. She couldn't hold them back anymore. She was lost to him, and it scared her. She hated this and loved it at the same time.

"Victoria?" he whispered. "Are you okay?"

"No." She brushed the tears away. "I'm tired, Matthew."

What she didn't say was she was tired of being alone. She was tired of fighting her feelings for him.

Matthew kissed her lips softly as he carried her to the bed.

They curled up side by side, and he ran his hands over her, stroking her.

"Why don't you sleep?" he asked.

"I don't want to sleep."

If she slept, then she'd wake up and the dream would end. It would all be over, and she didn't want that. She never wanted to wake up, so she kissed him again. Slow and lingering, igniting her desire, her need again. Matthew was the only one she wanted.

The only one.

She was ruined.

"Victoria, I can't get enough of you."

"Do you want me to stop?" she asked as she stroked him.

"God, no."

The rational part of her told her to end it, but she couldn't. She never wanted this to end. She wanted forever, but she was terrified by what that would mean. She was terrified of what might happen.

Matthew dozed off with Victoria in his arms. It felt so right holding her and being with her.

What're you doing?

He was setting himself up for heartache. The whole world now knew she had successfully done the domino surgery. It was only a matter of time before she headed back to New York. She'd made it clear that that was where her life was. And he didn't want his heart to be broken again.

He also wasn't sure he could ever take a chance on love again. Losing Victoria and Kirsten in one lifetime was enough heartache.

"You awake?" she asked.

"I am."

She sat up. "We havc to talk."

"I know."

She raised her eyebrows. "Do you?"

"New York got ahold of you, didn't they?" A shiver of dread ran down his spine.

This was it.

He was expecting it, but he was angry it was here and happening again. She was choosing New York over him.

"Yes. They want me to come back as soon as possible. Apparently they have a domino they need me to organize."

"Right." He got out of bed and started pulling on his clothes. His stomach felt like a rock, and he cursed himself for getting wrapped up with her again.

He was a fool.

"Well, we both said this was temporary."

Victoria looked disappointed. "Right."

"When do they want you back?"

"There's a flight out in the morning."

"And what about the patients in the intensive care unit?" he asked coldly.

"What about them? They're stable and in a good hospital," she replied. "I told you I'd stay for the surgery. I did."

"Okay." He finished getting dressed.

"Okay?" she asked, sounding a bit confused. "Don't you want me to stay until the patients are more stable?"

"You don't need to. We can handle it."

"I think I should stay."

"Why? It's okay to go, Victoria. I'm giving you an out. I mean, that's what you want. You want an out."

Although he didn't want her to take it, he couldn't ask her to stay, not when he knew she didn't want it. He could see that. New York came first; her career came first.

"An out? I see," she said quietly.

"Don't you want to go back to New York? That's what you've always wanted. That's why you ended things ten years ago."

"You know why I took that job! You grew up privileged with a family who loved you. I had nothing."

"I didn't know that then."

"You know it now. Nothing has changed, Matthew."

"Hasn't it, Victoria?"

"No. I have no one. I had no one."

"You had me."

"That wasn't enough." Her voice shook. "I needed that job."

"More than me."

"Yes," she admitted. "Love isn't a sure

thing. Besides, you didn't stay for me. You left me, too."

"Well, then you need to go back. New York is important to you. You don't need to worry about me. I moved on from you once before and I can do it again."

She pulled on her clothes. "That's it?"

"What more do you want?"

"I don't know. I didn't realize how much I had hurt you. I'm sorry."

"I'm okay," he said. "I'll be okay. I knew what I was getting into."

"I don't think you are. You've been hurt, and you lost Kirsten."

"Don't," he warned. "I'm fine. We didn't make any promises, Victoria. You're free to go."

She nodded, but her lips wobbled. "Well then, if I'm free to go… I will."

Victoria pushed past him and out of the on-call room.

His heart ached watching her leave. He didn't want her to go, but he couldn't let her stay here. This was not what she wanted.

New York City was all that mattered, and when she'd come here, back into his life, she hadn't hidden the fact that she wanted to go back as soon as she could.

He was giving her an out.

He was letting her go before he lost her.

Who says you'll lose her?

He shook that thought away. It was too scary to think about anything else. He was cursed when it came to love. He couldn't risk having his heart broken again.

Except that it was.

He still loved her. No matter how much he wanted to deny it, he'd always loved her, and he'd lost her again because he was scared.

Matthew wandered around the hospital for a long time—until the sun came up—thinking about everything, and finally made his way over to the floor where the domino patients were recovering from surgery.

He found his brother's room.

Marcus was sitting up, flicking through the television stations. Matthew walked into his room, and Marcus glanced over at him.

"Hey," Marcus said weakly. He looked pale, and as Matthew picked up his brother's chart, he could see Marcus had lost a lot of blood during the surgery.

His twin had almost died.

Someone else he had been pushing away for far too long.

"How are you feeling?"

"Great. Only because of the painkillers." He winced. "Vic did a great job."

"She did."

"What's wrong?" Marcus asked.

They used to be so close. He was tired of hiding from his twin. He'd missed too much trying to be his brother's keeper instead of being his brother's friend.

"Victoria and I had a fling ten years ago."

Marcus eyes widened. "What?"

"We were residents in Manhattan together. Both of us competing for the same position. She was offered it. She took it and ended our romance. I was broken."

"You loved her?" Marcus asked.

"I did."

Marcus tiled this head and studied him. "You still do."

"I do, but she doesn't love me."

"How do you know? Did you ask her?"

"No, but I know."

"I didn't realize you were omnipotent." Marcus smirked and then winced.

"I know. Trust me. Her career is the most important thing to her. She's going back to New York."

Marcus shook his head. "You're a chicken."

"Excuse me?" Matthew asked.

"Chicken. You're just making an assumption. Why did you leave her the first time? You could've stayed."

"You don't know what you're talking about."

"New York City is a big place. Why didn't you stay there? Get another job? Fight for her then? Instead you left and came home."

"Home is where I met Kirsten."

"And she was wonderful," Marcus said. "But she's gone, and she wouldn't want you to spend the rest of your life miserable. Of course, I've tried to tell you this time and time again, but you think I don't know anything."

"What do you know about love and loss? You bounce from woman to woman."

Marcus's eyes narrowed. "I've loved and lost before. Of course, you wouldn't know because you never talk to me. I've said it before and I'll say it again, you've tried to be my parent rather than my brother."

"I know," Matthew said gently.

Marcus winced, and Matthew checked his chart. He was due for some morphine in his intravenous line. He prepped the vial.

"Oh, great, now you're going to murder me," Marcus said dryly.

"They can detect morphine in an autopsy," Matthew teased, and they shared a smile as he injected the painkiller into his brother's line.

"Matthew, you love Vic. I think you always have."

It was a simple statement and something else he had been ignoring for so long. He'd thought if he ignored it, he could let go of that pain. It just didn't work that way, though. He'd met Kirsten and was glad for her—he'd loved her deeply—but he'd also never stopped loving Victoria.

His heart had never let her go, no matter how hard he'd tried.

He hated when Marcus was right.

"You're wiser than you let on, Marcus," Matthew teased.

"I know." He grinned, the morphine kicking in.

"I'm sorry I've ignored you and been so distant. You're right, I'm not your father. I will do better. We've missed too much time. I want to be your friend again. When I heard about your complication, I was scared."

"I want to be your friend, too. I don't want you to look out for me. I can take care of myself. I get on your nerves, but I care for you, Matthew. You've been miserable for five years. Just like you were miserable before Kirsten came into your life. I just want you to be happy."

"And if Victoria doesn't want me?"

"Then you'll know," Marcus said groggily.

"Thanks, bud. I'm proud of you, you know."

"Sure, tell me that when you know I won't remember," he mumbled.

Matthew chuckled. "Precisely."

Marcus drifted off to sleep, and Matthew stayed with him awhile before slipping out of his brother's room. He was terrified, but what Marcus had said made sense.

He loved Victoria.

He always had.

He could've stayed in New York, but he'd felt rejected and so he'd left. He was just as stubborn as she was. He didn't know what to do, but he knew one thing was for certain.

He loved Victoria.

Even after all these years, he loved her, and he was willing to get hurt if it meant a chance of having her again.

CHAPTER THIRTEEN

VICTORIA WAS WATCHING the rain out the window. She'd been back in Manhattan for the last three days, and it hadn't stopped.

Just absolutely poured down. It was miserable.

She never used to mind the drizzly weather when she was in New York, but now she missed the sun and sea of St. Thomas, wishing for the green and vibrant colors over the concrete jungle that was currently her view.

Of course, she'd never really paid much attention to the weather when she was in New York—she was always too busy with work.

That's what you wanted.

She'd wasted so much time.

There was a knock at the door, and she turned to see Paul step into the meeting room where she was waiting.

"You looked tanned and rested!" he said brightly.

"Three days ago I did a grueling domino surgery. I'm hardly that rested."

"Well, you looked better than you did when you left," Paul stated.

"I was worried about my career when you suggested I leave and take your place in St. Thomas," she corrected him. "I'm sure I looked a little bit more stressed then."

"That may be, but what you pulled off in a third-world hospital was impressive."

Victoria frowned. "It's not a third-world country. It's part of the United States. You need to educate yourself, Paul. You sound ignorant."

Paul waved his hand. "Whatever, the point was the hospital doesn't have the same kind of facilities that we have here."

Victoria rolled her eyes. She used to listen to Paul so eagerly, but right now she couldn't believe the nonsense that he was spouting. Had she also sounded like that before? All stuck-up and full of herself?

"Ziese Memorial Hospital is state-of-the-art," she said, feeling the need to defend the hospital...and to defend Matthew. She needed to get back to work. If she threw herself into her work, then she could hopefully get her mind off Matthew.

She should've just stayed away from him. Then she wouldn't have realized how much she still loved him.

Even after all these years.

Why did you leave him again?

Victoria shook that thought away. It didn't matter. What was done was done. She'd walked away from him again, but this time it was him that had pushed her away. She'd tried to reach out and offer to stay longer, but he'd told her to go.

He'd let her know that he didn't want her. Just like what had happened with all her foster parents.

"When can I get back to work, Paul?" she asked.

"Well, we called you back to do a domino, but the board would like it if you could arrange an even bigger domino surgery!"

She was shocked. "An even bigger one?"

"More than six."

"I'm not sure that's possible. You can't always put those kind of transplant surgeries together. Sometimes the stars just align."

Paul frowned at her. "We're one of the best

hospitals on the Eastern seaboard. Everyone comes here for transplant surgery."

"Only the people who can afford it," she said quickly.

"That's why we're opening up spaces for pro bono cases. We want to widen our pool and have you build a domino surgical team that surpasses all other hospitals. Then everyone will forget what happened with the ambassador."

It was like a slap across the face. "You know that it wasn't my fault. You know the complications I encountered, and you know I didn't even want to do that surgery in the first place."

She had been pressured into it by Paul and the board. She could see it now.

And here they were bullying her into something again. Something she didn't want to do because it was for all the wrong reasons.

They didn't care about the patients.

Victoria crossed her arms. "I'm not sure I'm comfortable seeking people to put in a domino, as you suggest. UNOS might have a problem with that."

"Victoria, this is your chance to get back in the good graces of the hospital. The one that started your career. I showed you everything," Paul said, as if she was a naughty child. Well, she was done trying to make him proud of her.

She was done trying please him or impress him.

She was done trying to prove her worth to unworthy people.

She was done trying to hold on to this position she'd won, because she didn't feel like much of a winner right now.

"And I appreciate that, but I can't in good conscience do this."

"What are you saying?" he asked.

Her heart began to race. She wasn't sure what she was saying. This job was everything she'd ever wanted. This was what she'd worked so hard for since she got that first scholarship for medical school. This had been her sole purpose when she was an intern and had fallen in love with transplant surgery.

Victoria hadn't realized that during her years here she'd lost her passion and her love for the surgery and it had become something of a business.

And she hated that.

When did she get like this?

Even though it terrified her, she knew what she had to do. She had to take the risk.

"I can't do it, Paul."

"What do you mean?" he asked, still confused.

"I need the place I work at to support me. If the hospital is only going to support me if I do something specific, something I can't control and something I don't feel comfortable doing, then I have to ask myself, what am I doing here?"

And it was true. She didn't know what she was doing here. Something she never thought she'd say.

"Are you telling me you want to resign?"

"Yes." Her voice shook a little bit. She really couldn't believe she was doing this. Her whole life had been centered around keeping her job, because it was security. She only wanted to rely on herself, because then she would only have herself to disappoint.

Except she was realizing that was no way to live a life.

"Victoria, don't be hasty. Think this through."

"I have thought it through."

She just wished she had figured this out sooner.

"Victoria, see sense," Paul said.

"I have. I quit, and since I can't work out my notice because the board doesn't feel comfortable having me practice, except for doing what they want me to do, I guess I can leave now."

Her hand shook as she took off her identification card and set it down on the table.

Victoria held her head up high and marched out of the office. Her stomach was doing flip-flops, but she knew she was doing the right thing.

Matthew might not want her anymore, but she had to tell him how she felt. She had been a fool, but she was going to put some things right again.

She was going to fly back down to St. Thomas, march into Ziese Memorial Hospital and tell him exactly how she'd felt all these years.

If she wanted any chance at any kind of happily-ever-after, she had to stop being so scared of what might happen. Life was passing her by.

She'd been frozen for so long. She just hadn't realized it.

Victoria collected the rest of her belongings and walked out of the hospital. She hopped in the first cab she found, which dropped her off in front of her Central Park West apartment.

When she got out of the cab, her heart

skipped a beat to see Matthew leaning against the side of the building, his gaze focused on her.

"Matthew?" she asked in disbelief.

"Hi."

"How long have you been standing there?"

He glanced down at his watch. "A couple of hours. Well, I did wander around a bit. I kept coming back and checking with your door-man to see if you'd come back."

Her heart skipped a beat. "You were plan-ning to wait here all day?"

"If I had to." He smiled at her. "Would you like to go for a walk? The rain has stopped."

"Sure." She went up to her doorman, who gladly took the box of her belongings to hold in his office until she got back.

She and Matthew walked silently side by side down the busy sidewalk toward Central Park. The sun was peeking from behind the gloomy clouds.

"Why are you here?" she finally asked.

"Are you upset to see me?"

"No," she said. "Just...surprised."

"Well, I came to offer you a job. Seems my board was pretty mad at me for letting you go back to New York without at least mak-ing you an offer."

"You could've emailed your offer to me. You didn't have to come here."

"I know." He grinned. "Marcus also wanted me to pass on his appreciation for the minimal scarring you left on him. He's quite impressed with your work."

Victoria laughed. "That's a great compliment. I guess."

"From Marcus, yes. It really is."

"Have you two made amends?" she asked.

"Sort of. We have a long way to go, but I think we're on the right track."

"Did you really fly hundreds of miles just to offer me a job and tell me that you and Marcus made up?" she teased.

"And if I did, what would you say?"

"You're crazy!"

He smiled that half smile that she loved so much. "So are you."

"So why did you really come here?"

"I want my transplant surgeon back."

Her heart skipped a beat again. "Just your surgeon?"

"No," he whispered. "I want you back."

She swallowed a lump in her throat. Tears were stinging her eyes. "You want me back?"

Matthew took a step toward her and took her hand in his. "You're trembling."

"A lot has happened today," she whispered.

"I love you, Victoria. I have for a long time, and I shouldn't have left you ten years ago."

"You didn't leave me. I chose a job over you."

Matthew smiled at her, touching her face softly. "I could've stayed in New York. It's a big city. I could've gotten a job at another hospital to stay with you, but I left you. I abandoned you."

"You didn't. I pushed you away. I didn't want a relationship. I just cared about my job. If you had, do you think we would've stayed together? Our relationship started off as sex and competition. Hardly a strong foundation."

"It doesn't matter. I should've stayed. I loved you, and I didn't fight for you. I'm sorry."

A tear slipped down her cheek. "I'm sorry that I chose something superficial over you, because I love you. I've missed you, and I want to start a family with you. I want to be a family with you."

Matthew pulled her into his arms and kissed her.

She sank into him, her heart melting.

"I love you, too, Victoria," he said. "I'll go anywhere to be with you. Even here."

She shook her head. "I want to go back to St. Thomas and work with the best chief of surgery on the island."

He grinned. "Deal, but I have one condition before I can offer you the job."

"Oh?" she asked, curious. "And what's this one condition?"

"Marry me."

"Well, I think that I can take the job with that condition."

Matthew kissed her again. "I love you, Victoria."

"I love you, Matthew."

She took his hand, and they walked back to her place. She was ready to leave New York behind and start her life anew in paradise.

EPILOGUE

One month later, St. Croix

MATTHEW STOOD WAITING for his bride-to-be. His pulse was racing, not because he was nervous, but because this was all he'd ever wanted.

Just him and Victoria.

His parents were watching the wedding from their cruise ship. They'd offered to fly back, but he'd told them there was no need. His parents were loving and supportive, but it was better just him, Victoria, Marcus as their witness and the officiant. No fuss. Just a few people and a gorgeous view, as his parents had given their blessing to use their castle on top of the mountain for their very simple wedding. Not that having it at their castle was simple…

Marcus escorted Victoria out of the house, and Matthew's breath caught in his throat.

She wore a simple white sheath gown, but she was breathtaking because she was his. Marcus nodded, smiling behind his new beard that he'd grown during his recovery so Victoria wouldn't mistakenly try to kiss him again.

He looked like he was still having a bit of pain while he was walking Victoria down the aisle. It wasn't surprising, as he'd just had surgery a month ago, but Matthew knew Marcus's gift had given a family back a wife and a mother.

And that, to Marcus, was worth every ounce of pain.

Marcus handed Victoria off to him with a wink and sat down.

Matthew took her hand in his and found she was trembling.

"Are you okay?" he whispered.

"Never better." She beamed at him, her dark eyes twinkling as the sun set over the turquoise sea, filling the sky with pink and gold. It was the perfect night, and not because of the sunset, but because Victoria was finally his.

The officiant stepped forward and started speaking, but Matthew couldn't focus on the words coming out of the man's mouth. All he saw was Victoria.

"Do you, Matthew Frederick Olesen, take Victoria Elizabeth Jensen to be your lawfully wedded wife?"

"I do." And he slipped the wedding ring on her finger.

"And do you, Victoria Elizabeth Jensen, take Matthew Frederick Olesen to be your lawfully wedded husband?"

"I do." And she slipped a ring on his finger.

"By the powers vested in me by the United States Virgin Islands, I now pronounce you husband and wife. You may kiss your bride."

Matthew pulled her in his arms and kissed her as Marcus escorted the officiant out.

Matthew wanted his brother to go, too. He had plans for his wife, and they involved just the two of them, the hot tub and then the bed.

Marcus came back. "The officiant is gone."

"Thank you," Matthew said. "Are you heading back to your boat now?"

Victoria nudged him. "Be nice."

"I am!" Matthew said.

Marcus rolled his eyes. "I'm so happy for you both. You'd better take care of Vic, or I'll kick your ass."

Matthew snorted. "As if!"

"Hey, I may be minus one kidney, but I can still take you," Marcus said.

"There will be no ass kicking today," Victoria stated.

"Why? Because it's your wedding day?" Marcus teased.

"No, because you're still recovering from surgery and I don't want you to mess up my work," she said.

Marcus and Matthew laughed.

"Well, congratulations, guys. I'll come visit in a month or two." Marcus winked and left.

It was just the two of them now. Matthew pulled her close, and they started dancing without any music, just like they did on their first date after she'd come back into his life.

This time he didn't have to fight any of these feelings.

They were together.

Finally.

"Do you want to dance all night?" she asked, teasing him.

"No." And then he kissed her. "I thought we could take this to the hot tub."

She made a face. "That's probably not the best idea."

"Why?" he asked.

"Remember a couple of days ago when I was feeling sick?"

"Yeah."

She looked at him pointedly, expecting him to come to a conclusion, but he couldn't figure out what she was hinting at.

"Matthew, you're a doctor. Think about it."

"I know I..." He trailed off as everything clicked into place. "Are you serious?"

Victoria nodded and kissed him. "Yes. I'm about six weeks."

"Six weeks. That puts us at..."

"I think it happened in the on-call room after the domino surgery. If you recall, you didn't have protection, and the pill is not exactly one hundred percent reliable. We were in a bit of a celebratory, albeit sleep-deprived, mood that night."

"That was a night to celebrate," he said huskily.

"Are you happy? I know kids weren't in our plans right away."

"Ecstatic. I know my parents will be, too." He pulled her into a kiss.

"So since the hot tub is out, do you have any other plans for tonight?" she teased.

"Oh, yes. The hot tub was just plan number

one." Matthew scooped her up in his arms, and she laughed.

"So what are your other plans, then?" she asked, wrapping her arms around his neck.

"Just forever." And he kissed her, carrying her off to the pool house, where he planned to show her just what forever with him looked like.

They were finally a family.

Finally together.

Forever.

* * * * *

Look out for the next story in the
Caribbean Island Hospital duet

A Ring for His Pregnant Midwife

If you enjoyed this story, check out these
other great reads from Amy Ruttan

Falling for His Runaway Nurse
Falling for the Billionaire Doc
Twin Surprise for the Baby Doctor

All available now!